A DESTINY

BY

SHASHHII THIMAIYA

First Published in 2020

Becomeshakespeare.com
Wordit Content Design & Editing Services Pvt Ltd
119-123, 1st floor, Building No. J2, Wadala East,
Wadala Truck Terminal, Mumbai, Maharashtra 400037, India
T: +91 8080226699

ISBN - 978-93-90040-77-3

About the Author

A Political Science Honors Graduate from Bangalore University. After a short career with reputed multinationals; took to writing. Married with two daughters and two adorable grandchildren.

Dedication

To my daughters, Shubha and Shyama

CHAPTER 1

The sun was just setting in the distant horizon when Rao Bahadur wound up the day's work at the plantation, and he headed back home. He drove an old dusty jeep which was quite battered with age. And even though the weathered jeep guzzled fuel, the vehicle was rather sturdy as it could brave the rough terrain that led to the estate.

Rao Bahadur soon reached the manor, and he brought the jeep to a screeching halt at the portico before entering the house. He then took off his grey overcoat and hung the garment on the wooden coat stand, before removing the black felt hat from his head and placing the headgear upon the table. Though the wide brimmed hat was a bit too large for his face, the oversized headgear protected him from the harsh rays of the scorching sun.

He proceeded towards the bar and poured himself a drink. Rao Bahadur chose the finest whiskey from amongst the range of alcohol on display which he then topped with ice sans any soda as he liked his scotch on the rocks. A drink before dinner was a daily routine, and it was a habit that he had acquired a long time ago.

His family comprised of him and his daughter, Nita, as his wife, Uma, had passed away shortly after giving birth to their only child. Since he was loathed to have a stepmother rear his daughter, he never remarried. And Nita was raised by her nanny, Ganga, who tried to be a good mother figure to the motherless girl.

Dinner was the most important meal at the manor, and it was often the only time when father and daughter ate together. Nita was usually asleep when her father arrived for breakfast, and she was invariably not home for lunch.

Rao Bahadur, however, dined alone tonight as his daughter was not present at the dinner table.

As Nita had a slight touch of the flu, she had decided to stay in bed. And her light meal comprising of thin chicken broth and bread sticks was served to her in her room.

Rao Bahadur stopped by Nita's room after dinner to check on her. And he enquired about her health. "How are you feeling?" He asked his daughter; tenderly touching her forehead.

Nita's forehead was a tad warm to the touch.

"Well, I still feel quite sick despite remaining in bed all day," Nita replied.

"Did you check your temperature?"

Rao Bahadur asked his daughter.

"Yes, I did," Nita replied.

"And what was the reading on the thermometer?" He asked.

"It's 99.2 degrees Fahrenheit," Nita replied.

"And did you take a pill for the fever?"

"Yes, I did. I took a Crocin."

"Well, since it's only a slight fever, it should subside soon. And I'm sure you will be fine by the morning," Rao Bahadur stated, trying to comfort his daughter.

"I certainly hope so as I hate to be sick," Nita said.

"Well, I will allow you to get some rest, and I hope to see you well in the morning. I think I shall go to bed now as I am rather tired." Rao Bahadur bid his daughter goodnight before proceeding to retire for the night. And he was just about to step out of Nita's room when he felt a sudden sharp pain shoot up his left arm, and he winced with the pain.

"What's the matter papa? Are you alright?" Nita asked her father, when she noticed him grimace.

"I don't know. I suddenly feel unbearably hot, and there's a sharp pain that's shooting up my arm which seems to be radiating to my back as well. And I feel sick and light headed," Rao Bahadur said. He was sweating profusely, and rivulets of perspiration were running down his face. And before long, he was completely drenched in sweat.

"Do you want me to adjust the air conditioning?" Nita asked. "Perhaps that would help," she said.

"Yes…," her father replied.

Nita set the air conditioner to 15 degrees Celsius, and the room turned quite cold. But in spite of the temperature in the room dipping, Rao Bahadur, however, continued to sweat. His breathing became rapid and shallow, and he began to cough and gasp for air. And his eyes rolled up, and he turned a deathly pale before collapsing on the floor.

Nita got a terrible fright when she saw Rao Bahadur pass out, and she thought that her father was dead. She, however, had the presence of mind to check his pulse and to listen to his heart beat. She was relieved to see that her father was still breathing; albeit barely, and that his feeble pulse was very faint.

She ran out of the room to get help, and she called Ganga.

"What's wrong with the master?" Ganga asked when she saw Rao Bahadur lying unconscious on the floor.

"I don't know," Nita replied.

"I think you should call Dr. Gowda, and ask him to come and attend to your father," Ganga stated.

"I don't know if it's appropriate to call Dr. Gowda at this time as it is pretty late. And I am rather hesitant to telephone him at this hour," Nita replied.

"Time is of the essence here. And as this is an emergency, I'm sure Dr. Gowda will not object to being disturbed at this hour of the night," Ganga declared.

Dr. Gowda had just returned home after visiting a sick patient when he received Nita's call. "Hello Nita, is everything fine with your father?" He asked. "It's not like you to call so late at night."

"I'm afraid not, doctor. Papa is unconscious, and I can't seem to revive him," Nita answered. She was close to tears and was trying not to cry.

"Alright, now don't panic and try and stay calm. I will be there as soon as I can," Dr. Gowda replied.

Despite the late hour, Dr. Gowda responded to Nita's call. And he arrived at the manor as quickly as he could before he proceeded to examine Rao Bahadur. "I'm afraid your father has had a heart attack, and he needs to be taken to the hospital right away. I've already called for an ambulance, and it should reach here shortly," he stated after concluding his examination.

"Is papa going to die?"

Nita asked the doctor.

"I hope not," Dr. Gowda replied. He looked grim, and he hoped for Nita's sake that her father's heart attack would not turn out to be fatal. He had warned Rao Bahadur a number of times about the perils of working hard at his age, and he had told the latter that he was straining his heart. But Rao Bahadur chose to ignore his physician, and he had paid no heed to Dr. Gowda's advice; as a consequence of which he had suffered a heart attack.

The ambulance arrived shortly, and in spite of being unwell, Nita accompanied her father to the hospital. She rode in the ambulance with Ganga, while Dr. Gowda followed them in his car.

Rao Bahadur was taken to the Civil Hospital in Mercara. And though the hospital could not be compared to the super specialist city medical centers, it was, however, the best medical facility that the sleepy town could boast of. Rao Bahadur was wheeled into the Emergency Room on the third floor where a team of doctors attended to him. As his heart had stopped short of beating, it was a herculean effort for the medical team to revive Rao Bahadur before he was given a new lease of life. And after a fortnight's stay at the hospital, he was allowed to return home.

Dr. Gowda dropped by at the manor to check on his patient. He met Rao Bahadur in the study where they were served tea and biscuits by Ganga.

"How do you feel now?" Dr. Gowda asked Rao Bahadur as he enquired about his health.

"I feel absolutely fine. I told you there was nothing to worry as I am not likely to die any time soon, and my heart will continue to beat for a long time," Rao Bahadur answered.

"Well, I hate to have to disappoint you, but that's where you are wrong." Dr. Gowda stated.

"And what do you mean? I managed to pull through fine, didn't I?" Rao Bahadur reiterated.

"I'm afraid that's not quite the case. The truth is that you almost died, and it is nothing short of a miracle that you are alive today," Dr. Gowda replied.

"That's utter nonsense," Rao Bahadur exclaimed.

"As you're more a friend to me than a patient, I will be very honest with you. Your heart attack was near fatal, and most men in your place would probably be dead by now. And you should consider yourself lucky to be alive. Should you push yourself too hard, I fear you'll end up having another heart attack sooner or later. And the next time, you might not be so fortunate. You need to make some life changes before it's too late. And I would advise you to take it easy from now on. After all, overseeing a one hundred acre coffee estate is not an easy job, and you are well past your prime now," Dr Gowda stated.

"And what do you suggest I do?" Rao Bahadur asked.

"Well, I suggest that you hire a supervisor for the estate, and hand over the responsibility of overseeing the plantation to him."

"I can't think of anyone who is suitable for the job," Rao Bahadur stated.

"I can speak to my nephew in Bangalore if you like, and ask him to find someone for the job. And I'm sure he will find the right person for the post."

"I'm not so sure if that's what I want. I am rather reluctant to hire a helping hand as I wouldn't know how good they would be," Rao Bahadur said.

"How hard could it be to supervise the labor on the estate?" Dr. Gowda asked. "If you love your daughter and want to be around for her, you will heed my advice. Do it for Nita's sake since she needs you for a few more years. Don't deprive her of both parents so early in life," he said.

"Well, I need to give it careful thought as it's a major decision for me to take," Rao Bahadur replied. He was averse to the idea of handing over the reins of Golden Acres to a stranger. The plantation was his baby, and he was loath to entrust his baby into another's care.

"I'd like you to give my suggestion some serious thought as it's for your own good," Dr. Gowda averred.

Rao Bahadur discussed the subject with Nita over dinner that night, and he mentioned the conversation that he had with his physician earlier in the day. "Dr. Gowda feels that I am too old to take on the responsibility of the plantation any more. And he suggested that I hire an overseer to do the job." He said to his daughter. "And what do you think I should do?" He asked Nita.

"Well, to be very frank, I think that you should heed Dr. Gowda's advice and consider appointing an overseer for the estate. Overseeing such a vast plantation is an exhausting job, and you don't have that kind of energy any more. And besides, you are no longer young," Nita said.

"Is that how you feel?"

Rao Bahadur asked his daughter.

"Yes, absolutely," Nita reiterated.

CHAPTER 2

"My nephew, Prem, has found the perfect candidate for the post of an overseer. But the only drawback being he lacks any work experience."

Dr. Gowda said to Rao Bahadur.

"Are you quite certain that the young man will be able to do justice to the job given that he has never worked on a plantation before? And considering that he lacks any experience, do you think he would be able to perform?" Rao Bahadur asked Dr. Gowda. "I am rather skeptical of hiring an inexperienced hand," he said.

"Prem assures me that Amar is willing to learn from scratch," Dr. Gowda replied. "And you should dispel any pre-conceived notions about him."

"And what about his credentials, do I know who I am hiring?"

Rao Bahadur queried.

"Well, his reputation is impeccable. And Prem vouches for his credibility. He assures me that Amar is a man of integrity."

"Well, since I have your word for it, Amar can be told that he has been hired. And I'd like him to join my services at the earliest," Rao Bahadur affirmed.

#

Amar Deep was hired for the post of overseer. And in spite of his lack of experience, he was recruited sans an interview solely on the recommendation of Dr. Gowda.

Amar was of dubious parentage. His mother, Maya, was a Madame who ran a successful escorts service in Bangalore, while his father, Randeep, was serving time in Bangalore Central Jail for murder. However, despite his tainted lineage, Amar was held in high esteem since his conduct was impeccable, and he commanded the utmost respect. And, fortunately for him, the stigma of his parents was not attached to him.

Amar arrived at the manor one Sunday morning while the family was at breakfast. And he introduced himself to his prospective employer.

"I hope you did not have any problem getting here?" Rao Bahadur asked Amar. "People tend to find it difficult to reach this place."

"No, fortunately I managed to find my way here without much difficulty," Amar replied.

"That's good. Are you hungry? Or have you eaten along the way considering that you've had a rather long journey?"

Rao Bahadur asked Amar.

"As a matter of fact, I am rather famished," Amar stated.

"Then I suggest that you join us for breakfast."

Rao Bahadur invited Amar to the breakfast table.

Nita was instantly attracted to Amar, and she was drawn towards him. She found him to be very good-looking, and her eyes often kept wandering in his direction as she could not quite resist glancing at him every now and then. And she found herself blushing when their eyes met briefly before he turned to address her father.

The housekeeper showed Amar to his quarters after breakfast. Amar's accommodation was a stone's throw away from the manor, and his living quarters was a cute little cottage that was nestled in a beautiful rose garden. And as the roses were in full bloom, the fragrance of the flowers filled the air.

Amar now began to have second thoughts about taking up the assignment, and he wondered whether he had made a mistake by accepting this job. As he was raw and inexperienced, and a complete greenhorn, he was not quite sure that he would do justice to the job.

#

A casual chat over a cup of coffee with Dr. Gowda's nephew, Prem, had landed him the job.

Prem and he were at the Koshy's restaurant on Brigade Road when Dr. Gowda's nephew mentioned about a possible vacancy on an estate. And Prem stated the need of an overseer to supervise a coffee plantation in Coorg.

"My uncle has entrusted me with the responsibility of finding a suitable person for a job on a coffee plantation in Mercara," Prem stated. "Do you know anyone?" He asked.

"Well, what about yours truly?" Amar said.

"What do you mean?" Prem asked.

"Well, I'd be interested in taking up the job," Amar stated.

"Are you serious?" Prem asked. "It's a one horse town and you'd soon be bored to death out there," he said.

"Yes, I'd be interested in giving the job a try," Amar reiterated.

Amar asked Prem to get in touch with his uncle before he found himself hired by Rao Bahadur.

#

Rao Bahadur showed Amar around the estate the following morning. As the estate was Amar's responsibility from now onwards, he would be required to oversee the plantation, and to supervise the labor from henceforth. Rao Bahadur let Amar take the wheels of the jeep, and he allowed his overseer to drive the vehicle as the latter would be required to handle the automobile from now on.

They returned to the manor for lunch. Rao Bahadur was surprised to see Nita join them at the dining table. As his daughter usually spent the day with a friend who lived close by, she was seldom home for the afternoon meal.

"I didn't expect you to be at home this time of the day, and I thought you would be with Meena."

Rao Bahadur said to his daughter.

"As a matter of fact, I was supposed to go over to Meena's place today, but she seemed to have other plans for the day," Nita replied.

"Anyways, it's always nice to have your company," Rao Bahadur stated.

As Amar was in a hurry to return to the cottage after lunch, he left soon after the meal. "May I be excused?" He asked Rao Bahadur. "I'd like to get back to my quarters."

"Yes, of course," Rao Bahadur replied.

Once he had returned to the cottage, Amar called his mother, Maya, in Bangalore.

"Hello mamma, I called to tell you that I've reached safely."

"I'm glad to hear that you had a safe journey as I was rather worried about you. Indian highways are virtual death traps, and I feared for your safety," Maya said. "By the way, how do you like your job? And how are you able to manage given that you have no previous work experience of any kind?" She asked her son.

"Well, it's not that bad, and besides, it's too early to tell," Amar answered.

"And how is your employer? Is he a kind man, and does he treat you well?" Maya queried.

"Yes, mamma, you've no cause for any worry. I am treated well, and I'm more like a member of the family than an employee. And I consider myself fortunate to get such a kind employer," Amar replied.

"And what about your meals, how do you manage for food considering you cannot cook?" Maya asked.

"Well that's taken care of, and I don't want you to worry on my behalf," Amar stated.

"Does that mean you have someone to cook for you?" Maya queried.

"Well you could say that," he replied.

"I'm glad to hear that you have a cook as your meals were my major concern since I know what a fussy eater you are," his mother said.

"Alright mamma, I shall keep in touch and update you of my welfare from time to time. And you take care of yourself."

Amar ended the conversation.

#

Amar had all his meals at the manor. Rao Bahadur and his daughter were gracious in their hospitality towards him, and he was treated like a part of the family. He had Nita's sole company at dinner one night as her father was not present at the table.

"Where's your father? Is he not eating tonight?"

Amar asked Nita.

"Papa has gone to the local club with a friend, and he will have dinner there," Nita replied; explaining her father's absence.

"I was afraid that your father had taken ill. And I was rather concerned about him," Amar said.

"Papa is taking good care of his health nowadays. And he is religiously following Dr. Gowda's advice," Nita said.

"That's good," Amar averred.

"I hope you like the meal. The cook had an emergency, and Ganga took over the kitchen today."

"Yes, it's fine, thank you," Amar replied.

Amar waited until Nita had finished her meal before he rose from the table. "I think I shall return to the cottage now," he said.

"Are you sure you want to return to the cottage right away?" Nita asked Amar. "You could join me in the lounge if you like," she said.

"Are you quite sure it's alright for me to stay back considering that your father is not around?"

Amar asked Nita.

"That's alright, and besides it is not very late," Nita answered. "Perhaps we could watch a movie."

"Well, that's not such a bad idea after all," Amar affirmed.

They proceeded to the lounge together where they made themselves comfortable on the couch.

Nita went through her father's collection of DVDs before selecting an old English classic. "I hope you like watching English movies of the earlier generation." She addressed Amar.

"Well, that depends; although I am not a great fan of English classics," Amar replied.

"How about "Gone with the Wind"? It's one of my favorites."

"Well then, that's quite a coincidence, since it is a timeless classic which happens to be one of my favorites too," Amar replied.

Nita inserted the disc in the DVD player but even before she could press "Play", Ganga arrived in the room. And she objected to Nita being alone with Amar.

"Don't you think it is getting rather late? It's time master Amar got back to the cottage." Ganga addressed Nita.

"Nonsense, we always spend time together after dinner. And why should it be any different today just because papa is not here," Nita replied. She was annoyed with Ganga for telling her what to do as it was not her nanny's place to lecture to her. Although Ganga had raised her since she was an infant, she was after all not her mother. And Nita had never accorded her nanny a mother's right.

"It's not right for a young lady to be with a man this late at night," Ganga reiterated.

"That's the most ridiculous thing to say as Amar is no stranger. In fact, he is practically a part of the family, and we will be fine on our own." Nita dismissed Ganga before settling down to watch the film. And as the picture was rather long with two intervals, it was close to midnight when the film finally ended.

"Gosh, I didn't quite realize how late it was. I really should get going now," Amar stated, rising from the couch.

"Amar, wait. Don't leave just yet." Nita stopped Amar even before he could depart for the cottage.

"Yes Nita, do you need something?" Amar asked.

"No, not really, but there is something that I need to tell you though," Nita replied.

"Alright; go ahead."

"I don't know if I will get another chance as papa is always around," she stated.

"Alright, I'm listening. And make it quick. It's really very late and your father won't be too pleased to see me here at this hour."

"I love you."

Nita confessed her love for Amar, and she told him that she had fallen for him.

"What? Do you realize what you just said?"

Amar asked Nita.

"Yes, that I love you," she reiterated.

"I really must go now," he stated, paying no heed to her confession.

"I fell in love with you the moment I saw you," Nita continued.

"You don't know anything about me," Amar said.

"And I don't care. All I know is that I love you. And I know that you love me too," Nita declared.

"No, I don't. You are mistaken. Good night."

Amar curtly dismissed Nita before leaving for the cottage.

#

Rao Bahadur greeted Amar when he arrived for breakfast the following morning.

"Good morning. It seems to be a bright day today as the sun is shining in all its glory," Rao Bahadur stated.

"Yes, it is, indeed," Amar replied.

Nita was not present at the dining table. Her chair remained vacant and a place had not been set for her. As she had changed her routine since Amar had arrived at Golden Acres, Nita usually joined the duo for breakfast.

"Is Nita not having breakfast today?" Amar asked Rao Bahadur, noticing her absence at the table.

"No, she got herself a ride into town, and she decided to skip breakfast today," Rao Bahadur replied.

Amar was afraid that Nita had done something foolish and stupid, and he was relieved to know that she was alright. He was caught completely unawares by Nita's confession last evening, and he had spent a sleepless night pondering upon what had transpired between them. He heard Nita sob, and he had caught a glimpse of her tear streaked face before he stepped out of the door. And his heart broke when he heard her muffled cry. Amar too was hurting just as much as Nita and it was a herculean effort to stop himself from taking her in his arms and kiss her tears away. He had fallen in love with Nita at the very first instant itself, and it was love at first sight for him as well. He had, however, maintained his distance with Nita as he did not quite trust himself with his emotions. And he feared that he would give in to his feelings. It had taken all his strength last night not to give in to the temptation of succumbing to Nita when he desperately desired to take her in his arms and crush her soft lips against his, and spend the night making tender love to her. And in spite of being madly in love with Nita, he chose to spurn her as he was well aware that Rao Bahadur would never allow his daughter to get involved with his overseer. And since he did not wish to have his heart broken, Amar decided to nip their love in the bud.

Amar and Rao Bahadur settled down to a game of poker in the study after dinner that night. And even though Nita's father was the occasional gambler, he, however, opted to play for no stakes in this instance.

"Let's not bring cash to the table," Rao Bahadur stated since he was loath to gamble.

"Yes, and I couldn't agree with you more. Let us not play for stakes," Amar replied.

Nita came to remind her father about his medication. She knocked gently on the study door before entering. "It's time for you to take your medicines papa," she said, handing her father his prescription pills along with a large glass of water.

"My daughter mothers me, and she takes real good care of me. I don't know what I will do once she gets married and goes away," Rao Bahadur said, gazing tenderly at Nita.

"I will never leave you," Nita retorted.

"Nonsense, every girl has to get married someday as her place is in her husband's home," Rao Bahadur stated.

"And I will ask my husband to move into the manor with me," Nita answered, much to her father's amusement.

"Well, I shall go to bed now. You two enjoy yourselves. The night is still young and it's too early for your bed time. Nita will walk you to the cottage as she could do with the night air."

Rao Bahadur addressed Amar.

"That won't be necessary," Amar stated. He was crazy about Nita, and he did not quite trust himself to be alone with her. And the last thing that he needed was for them to be thrown together.

"These grounds are very safe, and Nita will come to no harm," Rao Bahadur stated.

"That's not what I was afraid of."

"Do you find my daughter's company offensive?"

Rao Bahadur asked Amar.

"No, not all," Amar replied.

"Good, that's settled then. I will see you in the morning."

Rao Bahadur bid the duo goodnight before proceeding to his room.

They left for the cottage shortly after Rao Bahadur had retired for the night. As Nita did not wish to keep pace with Amar, she walked slightly ahead of him. And though she appeared to be unruffled by his presence, her calm demeanor, however, belied her pounding heart. Nita tried to convince herself that she hated Amar, but without much success. Her heart beat a trifle faster, and her pulse quickened at the mere sight of Amar as she was madly in love with him. And she wanted him to reciprocate her love. Although Amar had spurned her advances the night before, she was not deterred by the rebuff. And she wanted to see whether he would shun her again. Open doors tempt a saint they say, and even a saint could be lured to succumb to temptation. Nita wanted to put Amar to the test to see whether he was strong enough to resist her for a second time. And should she allow this opportunity to pass, she would regret this moment for as long as she lived.

Nita stopped walking, and she halted in her track. And she allowed Amar to catch up with her before she reached out to his hand, and took it.

Amar's heart skipped a beat at Nita's touch, and this time he did not spurn her. He took her in his arms and embraced her, before seeking her lips and kissing her passionately on her mouth.

"I love you. And I am so sorry that I hurt you last night," Amar mumbled against Nita's lips.

"Sh....Sh....," Nita silenced Amar even as she responded to his kiss.

They made love that night right there under the star studded sky. And the stars above were mute witness to their love making. As Amar tenderly deflowered Nita, he tried not to hurt her and cause her too much pain. And as Amar made love to Nita, she stopped herself from crying out at the immeasurable pleasure that was mingled with the exquisite pain.

#

Nita woke up feeling bilious, and when she tried to get out of bed she fell back on the pillow as she was dizzy, and her head was spinning like a top. And she lay down until the dizzy spell abated before she rose and wend her way to the bathroom. She was horrified when she retched and threw up all over the sink. She was well aware of what the symptoms meant, and she was dismayed to learn that she was pregnant. And she found herself in quite a quandary when she discovered that she was expecting Amar's child.

She considered taking Ganga into confidence, and she toyed with the idea of confiding in her nanny about her delicate condition, before she realized that she was foolish to even harbor such a thought. Although her nanny loved her like a daughter, Ganga's loyalty, however, lay with Rao

Bahadur since she owed allegiance to him. And Ganga would not hesitate to betray Nita's trust by informing her master about his daughter's condition. As Rao Bahadur cared deeply about his reputation, he would not forgive his daughter for disgracing him and for bringing shame to the family by having a child out of wedlock. And the consequences would be rather disastrous.

As Amar was the only person who Nita could trust, she decided to take him into confidence. And she mulled asking him to seek her father's permission to marry her. Although Rao Bahadur would be averse to the idea of Nita marrying Amar, and he would be loathed to have his overseer for a son-in-law, however, once he realized how much the two loved each other, he would bestow his blessings upon the duo.

Nita sought out Amar later that morning, and she cited the predicament that she found herself in. "I don't know how to tell you this as I've no idea how you will react. I am pregnant." She said to Amar.

"I'm sorry, but what was that again. I wasn't listening," Amar stated. He appeared to be rather distracted, and did not pay much attention to what Nita just said.

"I said that I am pregnant…," Nita reiterated.

"Are you serious?" Amar asked.

"Yes, I'm afraid so," she stated.

"Does anyone else know about this, and by that, I mean, Ganga; for instance?"

Amar asked Nita.

"No, and I wouldn't dare tell her since she would inform papa. You are the only one I can trust," Nita replied.

"And what do you suggest I do?" He asked.

"Perhaps you could talk to papa, and ask for my hand. And we could get married," she answered.

"And do you think your father would be willing to accept me for your husband?" He queried."After all, I'm his hired hand."

"Well, papa has no choice in this instance," Nita stated.

"I'm not so sure about that."

"I know papa. And he only wants my happiness, no matter at what cost."

"I hope you are right."

"Absolutely," Nita affirmed.

"Well then, can I count on you to hold on for a few more days?" Amar asked.

"What do you mean?"

Nita asked Amar.

"I have more pressing issues presently. You see my mother has met with a serious road accident and is grievously injured, and she is not expected to survive. And mamma is asking for me since she wants to see me before she passes away. As mamma does not have much time, I need to leave for Bangalore immediately. And I'm sure you understand my dilemma. However, I promise I'll get back as soon as I can and take care of everything," Amar said.

"I'm really scared as papa will throw one hell of a fit when he finds out that I am pregnant. He cares deeply about his reputation, and he will never forgive me for tarnishing his name," Nita stated..

"Do you trust me or not?" Amar asked.

"Yes, of course, I do," she answered.

"Then, just hang in there till I get back, and I'll sort things out once I am here. And I assure you that everything will be fine. Take care of yourself and our baby until then. Now, I suggest that you get back home before your presence is missed as I get the impression that Ganga keeps a tab on you." Amar kissed Nita lightly on the lips.

"Don't pay any heed to Ganga. As she has raised me since I was an infant, she tends to be overprotective of me," Nita replied.

"Well, I'm not so sure about that. I have the feeling that Ganga has a suspicion about our relationship," Amar reiterated.

Amar left for Bangalore shortly after Nita had met him. And a taxi was hired to take him to his destination.

#

Nita missed Amar terribly after he was gone, and she wondered how she would survive without him. She had grown accustomed to his presence in her life, and she now felt that a part of her was missing. And there was a terrible void without Amar. Each passing day sans Amar seemed like an eternity, and she felt his absence keenly.

She left the dining table mid-way through breakfast one morning, and she rushed to her room where she threw up in the bathroom sink. And she cried in her misery as she felt utterly helpless and alone. She had heard old wives' tales of raw papaya causing a miscarriage, and she wondered whether it really worked. And even though the thought was rather absurd, she was tempted to try out the remedy as she was quite desperate.

#

Amar did not arrive on the designated day that he was expected to report back to work, and Nita was tormented by angst and worry. She contemplated asking her father about his itinerary before she thought the better of it. Her father would find her curiosity about the overseer rather strange, and Rao Bahadur would wonder why Nita was interested in knowing the whereabouts of his hired help.

Amar, however, showed up a day later. He arrived the following morning, and he appeared to be in good spirits.

"You look rather cheerful and well," Rao Bahadur remarked, when he saw Amar.

"Well, I have good reason to be happy as my mother has managed to recover from the accident, and she is now back at home. Mamma's dramatic recovery left even the doctor's surprised, and they attributed her turnaround to divine intervention. And they termed her recovery as nothing short of a miracle."

"And I'm glad to hear that your mother is alright," Rao Bahadur stated.

Nita was pleased that Amar had returned, and she could not quite contain her joy at seeing him. "I'm so glad that you are back," she gushed, greeting Amar, and she was beaming with happiness.

Rao Bahadur was taken by surprise at his daughter's reaction to his overseer's return, and he wondered whether there was more to the friendship than met the eye. He tried to gauge Amar's response to his daughter's greeting, but the latter's demeanor was inscrutable.

Nita went to meet Amar at the cottage after dinner that night, but she was surprised to find the place in complete darkness. The lights had all been switched off, and it was so eerily quiet that the pregnant silence could be sliced through with a knife.

Amar usually left the lights on in the cottage, and the loud music playing on his stereo could be heard well beyond the gate. Nita presumed that Amar was tired after the long journey, and that he had retired early for the night. And since she did not wish to disturb him, she decided to return the following morning. However, even as she contemplated turning back and returning home, she longed for the comfort of Amar's arms, and she yearned to be snuggled in his warm embrace. And she could not wait to be with him again. Nita walked through the open gate, and she approached the cottage, but even before she could ring the door bell, she noticed the large padlock on the door. The cottage was locked from the outside, and Amar did not appear to be at home.

She turned back to return to the manor. And while proceeding to her room, she noticed that the lights in the study were on, and she heard voices coming from within. Seeing that her father was still awake, she stopped to wish him goodnight before retiring for the night. Nita knocked gently on the study before entering the room, but when she turned the knob, she found that the door was locked from inside.

Rao Bahadur never locked the study door unless he was in a serious discussion and he did not want to be disturbed. And this appeared to be one of those occasions when he wished to be left alone. Although Nita wanted to wait until the visitor had left; since she had no idea how long the meeting would last, she went to her room without seeing her father.

Nita woke up later than usual the following morning, and for some inexplicable reason, she had a sinking feeling. And she had an awful premonition that the day would not bode well for her. She went through her morning ablutions before proceeding for breakfast. And when she arrived at the dining room, she found that the table had been set only for two whilst the third place was missing.

Amar's place was empty, and the table had not been set for him. Nita wondered whether he had decided to skip breakfast, and she mulled asking her father the reason for his overseer's absence at the breakfast table this morning. However, even before she could ask her father about Amar, Rao Bahadur furnished the answer to her unasked question.

"Our overseer, Amar Deep, left our services late last night. And his decision to quit took me completely by surprise as it was very sudden, and he did not give me any prior notice," Rao Bahadur said.

CHAPTER 3

Rao Bahadur set about getting Nita married shortly after Amar had left their services. He scouted around for a suitable match for his daughter, and he spread the word amongst family and friends that he was looking for a groom for Nita. Rao Bahadur sought the help of his cousin, Cheema, and he asked the latter for his assistance in his quest for a son-in-law. Cheema had played the role of matchmaker in many an instance and was instrumental for the fruition of the alliance.

"Cheema, I am getting old now, and would like to see Nita married before I die. And I would appreciate it if you could find a good match for her." Rao Bahadur broached the topic of his daughter's marriage with his cousin.

"Don't you think that Nita is too young for marriage?" Cheema asked Rao Bahadur. "Perhaps, you should wait for a few more years before you decide to get her married," he said.

"Uma gave birth to Nita when she was her age," Rao Bahadur replied.

"Times were different then. I think you should seek Nita's opinion and see what she has to say before you arrange to get her wed," Cheema said.

"Nita is too immature to have an opinion, and she doesn't know what's good for her," Rao Bahadur answered.

"Is that how you feel?" Cheema asked.

"Yes," Rao Bahadur affirmed.

"Well, I suppose you know what's best for Nita since you are her father."

"Yes, absolutely," Rao Bahadur averred.

"Would you be interested in an alliance from overseas?" Cheema asked Rao Bahadur. "There is someone I know residing in the USA, and his father is seeking an alliance for him."

"No, I don't want an NRI groom for my daughter as I've heard that some of them already have foreign wives, and the Indian bride is treated like a slave," Rao Bahadur stated. "And I would much rather prefer an alliance from India."

"Well, in that case, I do have a boy in mind, and he is presently home on a holiday. But the only problem is that he is a widower," Cheema stated.

"Then you can rule him out, as he would probably be too old for Nita."

"How old is Nita?"

Cheema asked Rao Bahadur.

"Nita turned eighteen a couple of months ago," Rao Bahadur said.

"Well, Rohit is in his mid twenties, so there won't be too much of an age difference between the two. And besides, he is doing very well for himself," Cheema said.

"Can you cite his credentials?"

"Rohit is an MBA from America, and he is presently employed with Stan Express Bank at their Mumbai Headquarters. And he has recently been promoted as Vice-President," Cheema said.

"Well, Rohit's credentials appear to be pretty impressive. Perhaps, I could meet him with an open mind, and see how it goes from there." Rao Bahadur evinced interest in the alliance.

"Alright then, I shall endeavor to fix a date and time that's suitable to both the families. And I hope everything works out well. And where would you like the meeting to be arranged?"

Cheema asked Rao Bahadur.

"I feel that your residence would be the ideal place for us to meet since you are the common factor between the two families."

"Alright then, I shall get in touch with you shortly," Cheema affirmed.

Rao Bahadur heard from Cheema a couple of days later. "I've arranged for the two families to meet at my place on Sunday for lunch. The ambience will be informal, and there will not be any awkwardness."

"That's fine by me. And what time is lunch?" Rao Bahadur asked.

"Lunch is around 2.00 P.M. but I suggest that you arrive by 12.00 noon."

Rao Bahadur arrived at Cheema's residence along with his daughter shortly after 12.00 noon on the designated day. They were met by their host who introduced the two families to each other.

"This is my cousin who I spoke to you about. And this is his daughter, Nita," Cheema stated, completing the formalities of the introduction.

#

Rohit was wary of meeting a prospective bride as he had bitter memories of his earlier marriage. Rani and he had a traditional arranged marriage, and the relationship was volatile from the very start. His wife and he could not see eye to eye on just about anything, and they invariably found themselves having a verbal duel. Rani accused Rohit of being an abusive husband among other things, and she resented being kept under his control. Things came to a head one night when Rohit raised his hand on his wife in a fit of rage, and he resorted to physical violence. And even though he regretted his transgression in the very next instant, and he was profusely apologetic for his brutality, Rani, however, was in no mood to forgive him. And she punished him in the most macabre manner. Rani took an overdose of sleeping pills that night, and Rohit found his wife lying dead next to him the following morning. Rani's parents blamed Rohit for their daughter's suicide, and they threatened to take legal action against their son-in-law, before they were adequately compensated.

He was, however, awestruck by Nita, and he was glad that he had agreed to meet her. Nita was ethereally beautiful, and she possessed an air of innocence. And she was a far cry from his worldly-wise late wife. Rohit found himself charmed by this child-woman, and he decided to give marriage a second chance.

"Well, I have no objection to this alliance, and I am willing to marry Nita." Rohit consented to the match, before turning to his parents for their approval. "Are you happy with my choice of a bride or do you have any objection?" He asked his mother.

"We could not have picked a prettier bride for you." Rohit's mother said.

"As I'd like to take my bride with me when I report back to work after my vacation, I would prefer to have the wedding as soon as possible," Rohit stated.

"Yes, of course, I understand. The wedding shall be held at the earliest," Rao Bahadur affirmed.

"And I'm sorry if I come across as being too demanding, but I'd like to have a lavish affair together with all the pomp and show that go with the occasion even though this is my second marriage," Rohit said.

"You can rest assured that the wedding will be a grand affair," Rao Bahadur replied.

"And, pardon me for asking you this, but what about the dowry that you intend to give me?"

Rohit asked Rao Bahadur.

"It shall be an unmentionable sum, and enough to keep you happy," Rao Bahadur declared. He did not consult his daughter before giving his consent to the alliance, and he did not seek Nita's opinion before agreeing to the match. His daughter was expected to abide by his decision and do his bidding, and she would have to marry the man her father had chosen for her.

#

Nita had no inkling that she was coming to meet a prospective groom, and she was given to understand that this was a social visit. She realized that her father had deceived her, and that she had been tricked into presenting herself for the customary bridal inspection.

#

"I'm not ready to get married as I'm still too young."

Nita protested when she was told that she was wedding Rohit.

"Nonsense, many girls your age get married," her father stated.

"I don't know Rohit, and he is a complete stranger to me," she reiterated.

"For that matter, neither did your mother and I know each other before we got married. In fact, we didn't even see one another before the wedding as it was our parents who arranged the match." Rao Bahadur brushed aside his daughter's fears.

"Yes, I am aware that mamma and you were strangers before you wed, but you grew to love each other as time went by," Nita said.

"And, what makes you think that Rohit will not grow to love you?"

Rao Bahadur asked Nita.

"Well, for starters, I don't love him," she declared.

"You will learn to love Rohit in due time," her father averred.

"And, what if that never happens?" Nita asked.

"I can assure you that it is not going to be the case, and you will have a happy marriage," Rao Bahadur reiterated.

#

Nita was loathed to enter into matrimony with a complete stranger, and she wanted the wedding to be called off. And since her pleas to her father fell upon deaf ears, she turned to Ganga for help.

"I don't want to marry Rohit," Nita said to Ganga.

"And can you tell me the reason why you don't wish to marry him?" Ganga asked.

"I don't love Rohit," Nita stated.

"Love blossoms after marriage," Ganga said.

"Not in my case since my heart already belongs to someone else," Nita reiterated.

"And who does your heart belong to?"

Ganga asked Nita.

"My heart belongs to Amar," Nita replied.

"Well, Amar vanished overnight, and no one has heard from him since," Ganga said.

"Amar promised that he would be there for me. And he would never go back on his word," Nita reiterated.

"People make promises only to break them later. And it's the same with Amar as well. He made you a promise which he had no intention of fulfilling," Ganga stated.

"Well, whatever it may be, I refuse to marry Rohit. I tried reasoning with papa but he is not willing to listen to me. And you know how stubborn papa can be at times. I want you to speak to papa on my behalf, and convince him to call off the nuptials."

"And what makes you think your father will pay heed to me?" Ganga asked.

"That's because papa knows that you mean well for me," Nita replied.

"You're wasting your breath trying to tell me to talk to your father into calling off the wedding as I'll do nothing of the sort. And stop behaving like a child. You know that you have to marry some day, and Rohit is the perfect match for you. And don't you know that your father only has your best interest at heart?"

Ganga chided Nita.

"I wish mamma was alive today. She would never have allowed papa to force me into this marriage," Nita mumbled tearfully when she realized that her last hope of having the wedding called off was dashed to the ground.

#

Rao Bahadur invited practically the entire town to witness his daughter getting married, and he spared no expenses to ensure that Nita's wedding was a grand affair. Since he was giving away his only daughter's hand in marriage, he wanted her wedding to be an affair to be remembered long after the ceremony was over. His poorer kin, however, were omitted from the list of invitees, and those who gate crashed the wedding were allowed to remain at the venue, as it was considered inauspicious to turn them away from the joyous occasion.

Nita made a lovely bride, and she looked ravishing in her bridal finery. Her hands and feet were artistically hennaed, and the beautiful brocade sari which she wore was an heirloom that was passed down in the family for generations. The sari was passed down from mother to daughter, and Nita's mother had worn the same sari at her wedding, and her grandmother before that. The jewelry that she wore was worth a small fortune. And it had been inherited by her mother from her grandmother, and it was now passed on to Nita.

She remained composed during the ceremony, and no one had any inkling that she was a reluctant bride. She was given away in marriage to Rohit by her father who performed the kanyadhan or the gifting of the bride to the groom.

The nuptials soon came to an end, and it was time for the bride to depart from her parental home.

Rao Bahadur could not contain his tears when he bid Nita goodbye, and he wept bitterly as he hugged her. His heart ached to let his daughter go. He would have liked to have waited for a couple of years before getting Nita married and burdening her with the responsibility of matrimony. The situation, however, demanded that Nita get married immediately, and he was compelled to get her wed at the earliest. He was guilty of forcing her into this marriage, and of getting her wed against her will. He hoped that his daughter would understand his predicament, and that she would be willing to forgive him some day. "I am going to miss you terribly, and the house will be empty without you," he said.

Nita was sobbing as she clung to her father, and she did not want to leave him. Rao Bahadur was the only parent she knew who had played the role of both a father as well as a mother in her life. And although her father had failed miserably on both counts, he had, however, done the best that he could. Nita was leaving familiar surroundings, and she was now entering into another home.

As she stepped out of the familiar comfort of her childhood home, the enormity of her new life dawned upon her. She was leaving behind her innocence, her girlishness and her childhood dreams, and she was now embarking upon a new beginning with a complete stranger. And even though the stranger was her husband it was of little consolation, since Nita would be setting up home with a man she barely knew.

Nita dreaded the nuptial night when she would be required to perform her duty as a wife and accord her husband his conjugal right. And she shuddered at the mere thought of fulfilling her spousal obligation. She was loathed to have Rohit touch her, and when her husband entered the room later that night she feigned deep slumber.

Rohit had desired Nita from the moment he had first set his eyes upon her, and he could not wait to have her. He began by gently caressing Nita's face and tenderly kissing her eyes, before crushing her soft lips against his. Rohit gradually undressed Nita and disrobed her, as he proceeded to remove all her garments until she lay stark naked before him. And he drank in every detail of his beautiful bride before making love to her. Nita, on her part, lay motionless, and she did not respond to Rohit's lovemaking as she felt violated and used by her husband.

CHAPTER 4

Jagdeep was recently diagnosed with cancer, and he was told that he was stricken with a life threatening disease. And since learning about his illness, he decided that it was time to bury the hatchet, and to make amends to his estranged son. When Vikram had set up home with a prostitute he was so incensed with his son that he severed all ties with the latter, and he had cut Vikram out of his life. He felt betrayed by his son for being with a fallen woman, and he loathed Vikram for tarnishing the family name. And Jagdeep disowned his only offspring. Even the news of Vikram's death did not move him enough to relent, and he refused to attend his son's funeral, and he declined to be present to conduct his last rites.

#

"Meher, I think it's time that we forgave Vikram, and stopped bearing a grudge against him for being with Maya," Jagdeep said to his wife over dinner one night.

"Yes, that's right. We can't hold it against our son for falling in love with the wrong woman, and for setting up home with her," Meher stated.

"And I know that it's too late to forgive Vikram as he's long dead and gone. But we could, however, make amends to his family."

"Yes you're right, after all Vikram's son is our grandchild," Meher replied. "And how do you hope to trace our son's family considering that we have lost all touch with Maya after Vikram's death?" She asked her husband.

"Well, I've Vikram's last known address in Bangalore, and let's hope his family still resides there."

"Since you've finally decided to bring Vikram's family into the fold, the sooner it's done the better," Meher said.

"Yes, I know. I'm thinking of leaving tomorrow itself," Jagdeep answered.

Jagdeep left for Bangalore the following morning. He took the first flight out of Mumbai as he was anxious to meet his grandson.

Once he had arrived at the garden city, he hired a taxi to take him to Richmond Town.

Jagdeep alighted outside Vikram's apartment building, and he dismissed the taxi before proceeding to the apartment on the 24th floor. He tentatively rang the door bell, and as he waited for the door to be answered, he rehearsed the speech which he would deliver to Maya. He would beg Maya for her forgiveness, and he would ask her to grant him a second chance to make reparations for the past.

The bell was answered shortly, and a stranger stood at the door.

"I am looking for the previous tenants who lived here. Do you know where I could find them?"

Jagdeep asked the present resident.

"I am sorry, but I've no idea where they currently reside," the lady of the house replied.

"Did they leave behind any forwarding address? Do you know where they have moved?" Jagdeep asked.

"No, I'm afraid not," the lady reiterated.

Jagdeep had failed to find Maya, and he had reached a dead end in his quest for her. Maya could be anywhere in this vast city, and sans a clue to her whereabouts, he was left stumbling in the dark. Since searching for Maya was akin to looking for a needle in a haystack; he realized that it was a colossal waste of time. And he reckoned that he was unlikely to meet with much success.

Sorely disappointed by the failure of his mission; Jagdeep returned to Mumbai with a heavy heart.

"Did you meet Maya and our grandson? And how are they?" Meher asked her husband. "I hope they are well."

"I'm sorry, but my trip turned out to be a complete waste, and I'm afraid I failed in my mission," Jagdeep replied.

"What do you mean?"

Meher asked Jagdeep.

"I didn't find Maya at Vikram's last address. And she appears to have moved out," Jagdeep said.

"And didn't you ask for her current address?"

Meher asked her husband.

"Yes, I did. But the current residents have no idea about Maya's whereabouts as she did not leave behind a forwarding address."

"That's a real shame, and I'm very upset with the turn of events. I was looking forward to meeting Maya and our grandson," Meher said.

"Well, I'm equally disappointed too," Jagdeep averred.

"I suppose we are being punished for being harsh on our son. And his only fault was to fall in love with a fallen woman," Meher said.

"Yes, you're right, and we probably deserve to be punished for being unduly severe towards Vikram when we should have been more accepting as parents. We were terribly selfish to hold our prestige over our son's happiness."

"Well, that credit goes to you," Meher replied.

"What do you mean?" Jagdeep asked.

"It was you who bore a grudge against Vikram for shaming the family, whereas I was only concerned with his happiness. And I was willing to accept Maya had it not been for you. It was only on account of you that Vikram was estranged from us," Meher said.

"I am aware of that, but what good does it do to rake up old issues?" Jagdeep asked.

"I should never have allowed you to coerce me into cutting all ties with my son," Meher replied.

"If I remember correctly; that decision was not mine alone, but yours too," Jagdeep said.

"And it was a decision that I was compelled to take under duress when you resorted to emotional blackmail," Meher replied.

"What do you mean?" her husband asked.

"I was reluctant to sever ties with Vikram. And when you realized that I was willing to extend the olive branch to him, you pleaded with me not to make peace with my son as it would kill you. And it was only the thought of losing you that compelled me to support your decision to be estranged from our only child."

#

Meher never wanted to cut ties with Vikram, and she loved him enough to overlook his failings. When Vikram brought Maya home to seek his parents' blessings, Meher was ready to accept her as family, and she was willing to give Maya a place in her heart. And she was prepared to accord Maya a warm welcome and to bestow her son's wife the honor of a daughter. However, when Jagdeep resorted to emotional blackmail, she found herself in a quandary. And when she was asked to choose between her husband and her son, with the former threatening to kill himself should she opt to side with the latter, she was caught in a dilemma. Faced with the bleak prospect of losing her husband; she was compelled to choose her spouse over her son. And even though her decision to sever ties with Vikram broke Meher's heart, she was forced to be estranged from him for the sake of her husband.

She never forgave herself for severing ties with Vikram and for turning her back on her son. And she felt that she had failed miserably in her duty as a parent. When Vikram died in a tragic road accident while still in the prime of his life, she had blamed herself for his death. She believed that her son had fallen an easy prey to dark forces as he had lacked his mother's blessing. Her son's untimely demise weighed heavily upon Meher's conscience until the guilt became too much for her to bear. And she sought to find solace in death.

Meher committed suicide one night after leaving behind a note for her husband. She filled the tub with hot water and stepped into the bath before taking a razor and slitting both her wrists until they bled. And as she watched herself bleed; her life slowly ebbed away.

Jagdeep found Meher drowned in the bath tub the following morning, and he discovered the letter which she had left behind for him.

"I am sorry for killing myself, but I could no longer live with the guilt of being responsible for our son's death. Since I believe that it is only because of me that Vikram is dead, I don't feel that I deserve to be alive. The only hope of forgiveness from our deceased son is to make amends to his family, and I don't want you to stop looking for them until they are found. Then and only then, will I be at peace."

Meher's suicide note read.

Jagdeep wanted to fulfill his wife's last wish to ensure that she would finally be at peace, but he was, however, skeptical of meeting with much success. And he resigned himself to the fact that he would never be able to trace his son's family or ever get a chance to meet them.

#

Amar's mother was dead. Maya had passed away a short while ago after a brief illness, and she was cremated the same day. Her funeral was a small affair with only a handful of people present at the electric crematorium to watch her being consigned to flames. Her ashes were collected the following morning by her son who immersed them in the holy river Sangam near Srirangapatna town before praying for the peace of the soul.

Amar was told about the truth of his family by his dying mother, and he was surprised to know that Randeep was not his parent as he had been led to believe, but that the latter was entrusted to play the role of his father in order to provide him with a normal home with two parents. Maya had met Randeep in a bar, and as he was homeless at the time, she had offered him shelter in her home in exchange for him donning the mantle of a father to Amar. Randeep, however, was loath to play the role that was expected of him since he despised Amar from the very start. And he lost no opportunity to ill-treat the latter before he was asked by Maya to leave their home after one such brutal incident. And ever since his incarceration, they had lost all touch with him.

His biological father, Vikram, was long dead, having died in a road accident while he was still in the prime of his life. And as Amar was a mere toddler at the time of his death, he had no memories of his father.

Maya was once a prostitute, and she had met Vikram in the line of her profession before they fell in love and decided to get married. And their union had incurred the wrath of his parents who sought to sever all ties with their son. Maya left her profession to switch to the role of a homemaker, until Vikram's untimely demise forced her to fend for herself and her son. And when she failed to secure a respectable job on account of her antecedents, Maya was compelled to set up an escorts service to provide for the family.

Amar's paternal grandparents resided in Mumbai. And although they were estranged from their son, his mother wanted him to get in touch with them after her death. Since Maya did not want her son to be sans a family after she was gone, she asked Amar to contact his grandparents, and to endeavor to win over their hearts.

#

Jagdeep was surprised to hear from Amar, and he could not quite believe that it was his grandson at the other end.

"Hi dadaji, this is Amar here. And I am your grandson."

Amar introduced himself to his grandfather.

"I never expected to hear from you," Jagdeep stated.

"You mean considering the bad blood between my father and you?" Amar said; referring to the strained relations between Jagdeep and Vikram.

"Yes," Jagdeep affirmed. "Although I realized later that I should not have been so harsh on Vikram, and I even came looking for you and your mother in Bangalore at your last known address but had to return home disappointed," he added.

"That's because we had to move out of the place as the landlord was threatening to have us evicted," Amar replied.

"And how is Maya?" Jagdeep asked Amar. "I hope all is well with her."

"I am afraid mamma is no more. She passed away a while ago," Amar replied.

"I'm sorry to hear about Maya. Her death must be hard on you," Jagdeep said. "You have my condolences." He offered his sympathy to Amar on the demise of the latter's mother.

"My mother was the only family I had. And I find myself all alone after she is gone," Amar stated.

"Don't ever feel that you are all alone as I'm still alive. And I am family too," Jagdeep said."By the way, why don't you come to live with me in Mumbai?" He asked.

"Are you quite sure that's what you want?" Amar asked.

"Yes, absolutely," Jagdeep affirmed.

"That's very kind of you, but then I wouldn't want to be a burden to you and daadi."

"Nonsense, our grandson would never be a burden. On the other hand, we would be happy to have you live with us," Jagdeep reiterated.

"What about daddi? Does she feel the same way too?"

"It's only me now since Meher has passed away. And had she been alive, she would've been more than happy to welcome her grandson into her home."

#

Amar soon wound up his affairs in the Garden City. He sold Maya's business at a considerable profit to an old acquaintance of hers. And he let out their apartment on Castle Street on a long term lease to a friend, before moving out of the city. He arrived in Mumbai in the midst of the summer when the city was at its sweltering worst. And after alighting at the domestic airport, Amar hired a radio taxi to ferry him to his destination.

"I need to get to Nepean Sea Road."

Amar instructed the taxi driver.

"Alright," the taxi driver stated, before accommodating his passenger in the cab.

As the taxi maneuvered through the crowded streets, and streamed in and out of the flowing traffic, Amar took in the sights and sounds of the city. This was his first visit to the commercial capital, and he was fascinated by the unending sea of humanity that thronged the busy streets.

#

Ridgeway Towers was a tall structure that was situated opposite the Priyadarshini Park, and the towering building rose to meet the Mumbai skyline. Jagdeep resided on the sixth floor, and his apartment provided him with a scenic view of the Arabian Sea.

Amar rode the express elevator to the sixth floor before ringing the doorbell to his grandfather's apartment. And he was a bundle of nerves while he waited for the bell to be answered. He could not help wondering whether his grandfather would be happy to see him, and whether he would be welcomed with open arms.

The door was answered shortly by a male servant who showed Amar inside the apartment.

"I'm so happy to finally get to meet you," Jagdeep stated, hugging Amar warmly. He was effusive in his affections, and he did not hold himself back.

"And the feeling is mutual since I'm glad I came," Amar replied. He was overwhelmed by Jagdeep's affection, and he was ashamed to have had any misgivings about his grandfather.

#

Jagdeep noticed that Amar was the spitting image of his late father, and he felt that his son had come back to him. He never stopped regretting his decision to be estranged from his son, and not a day went by that he wished he could turn back the clock. However, his arrogance prevented him from extending the olive branch to Vikram. And since he was loathed to swallow his pride, he had preferred to place a stone over his heart and decline to attend his son's funeral. Jagdeep now wished to make amends to Vikram through Amar, and he hoped that his son would finally forgive him.

Amar took very little time to adjust to his new life, and he played the role of devoted grandson to the hilt. And Jagdeep now had a shoulder to lean on in his old age.

Jagdeep and Amar soon became buddies, and they shared each other's joys and sorrows.

Amar was curious to know about his father. And he wanted to garner information about his parent from his grandfather. "I was too young to remember my father and have no memories of him. And mamma never ever spoke of him. Can you tell me about him?" Amar asked Jagdeep.

"Well, your father was a rebel who believed in living life on his own terms. And he didn't quite believe in subscribing to the norms of society. That's the reason why he didn't find anything wrong in being with someone like your mother," Jagdeep answered.

"And is that the only reason why you cut all ties with your son?" Amar asked.

"Vikram's mother and I were angry with him for showing no regard to our feelings. And we felt that we had been betrayed by our son," Jagdeep reiterated.

"And are you still angry with my father for what he did?"

Amar asked Jagdeep.

"No, as a matter of fact, I forgave Vikram a long time ago. After all, he was our only child. But then I let my pride get the better of me, and that stopped me from reaching out to him."

"And what about daadi, did she go to her grave still hating her son?" Amar asked.

"Meher's anger did not last long as a mother always forgives her child. And it was only the thought of offending me that stopped her from making her peace with Vikram. And that's what killed her," Jagdeep replied.

"How so?" Amar asked.

"Meher was wracked with guilt for turning her back on Vikram as she felt that his mother's ire had led to his untimely demise. And she never forgave herself for Vikram's death."

"And is that why daadi killed herself?" Amar queried.

"Yes, in fact, Meher committed suicide on Vikram's birthday."

"That's very tragic indeed," Amar said.

"I should have seen that coming. And in a way, I blame myself for Meher's death."

"How so?"

Amar asked Jagdeep.

"Meher was loath to turn her back on Vikram, and it was I who forced her to sever ties with our son."

"Dadaji, repentance cannot change the situation, so it's best to forget the past." Amar tried to console Jagdeep.

"I suppose you're right. I am not going to dwell on the past from now on since it's the present that matters, and I'm looking forward to our life together. There is so much catching up to do, and probably very little time," Jagdeep said.

"And what do you mean?"

Amar asked Jagdeep.

"I don't know how much longer I will live. After all, I'm an ill old man and could go any time without so much as a warning," Jagdeep answered.

"That's nothing but nonsense, and I am sure you will live for a long time," Amar said.

"And now that you are here with me, I don't want to die any time soon," Jagdeep stated.

"And, believe me, you won't. Besides, I'm looking forward to starting a new life with you," Amar reiterated.

"It's good to hear that. Let us make the most of the time we have so that there are no regrets. And I'm looking forward to seeing my great-grandchildren," Jagdeep said.

Amar updated Jagdeep about his life up until his arrival in Mumbai. He narrated to his grandfather the terrible tragedy that had befallen him, and he told the latter of how he had existed on the brink of extinction before being saved in the nick of time.

"I tried to kill myself at the time as I did not wish to live any longer," Amar stated, as he spoke about his attempted suicide.

"I can well understand your pain at what you've been through, but life is for living. You need to put the past behind you and look forward to the future as the future holds much promise," Jagdeep said.

CHAPTER 5

Nita moved to Mumbai after her marriage to Rohit, and she began a new life with her husband. She went from being a small town girl to a Mumbaikar, and she soon grew to love the bustling metro. She would often get lost amongst the milling crowds that thronged the busy streets, and at times, she went for a ride on the suburban railways. And she boarded the local trains for the sole purpose of experiencing the typical Mumbai life. Her favorite pastime was to sit on a bench at the railway platform, and to watch the people go by.

She had just entered Churchgate Station when she saw Amar dart across, and he was hurrying to catch the train. Nita could never understand why he had reneged on his promise, and she could not comprehend why he had vanished overnight. She was completely devastated by his sudden departure, and her world had come crashing down when he walked out on her and their child. She had trusted him with her life, but he had chosen to turn his back on her. And Amar's disappearance was a mystery to which she sought to get some answers.

Nita followed after Amar to speak to him, but even before she could catch up with him, she tripped on her toe and took a tumble, and she fell flat on her face. She, however, managed to recover instantly from the fall, and when she got back upon her feet again, she found that Amar had already boarded the train. She tried calling out to him to get his attention, but he did not hear her as the train had started to move before gathering speed and leaving the station.

#

Nita was having dinner with her husband later that night when she felt the faint stirrings of an ache in her belly. And before she knew it; a sudden sharp stab of pain shot up her stomach. The pain was so excruciating that Nita thought that she would die. And she turned pale as she blanched with the horrendous pain.

"Are you alright?" Rohit asked his wife, noticing her sudden pallor. "You look as white as a sheet," he remarked, commenting on her pallid appearance.

"I'm in acute pain," Nita replied.

"Could you think of anything that might have triggered the pain?"

Rohit asked Nita.

"Well, I took a tumble earlier in the day," Nita replied.

"And do you think that's what caused the pain?"

"I don't know since I was fine after the fall."

"Well, how bad is it? I mean do you want to go to the hospital right away? Or would you rather watch and wait until the morning?"

Rohit asked Nita.

"I think it would be better to get to the hospital right away instead of waiting until the morning," Nita gasped, as she felt a second sharp stab of pain. And this time the pain was far worse than the first, and Rohit's face appeared to swim before her eyes. "And I think I'm bleeding too," she added, as she felt a warm wetness pervade her panty.

Rohit took Nita to the Breach Candy Hospital on Warden Road where she was examined by the obstetrician.

"I am afraid you have suffered a miscarriage. And you've lost the baby," the gynaecologist stated.

Nita received the news of her miscarriage with mixed emotions, and she did not know whether to feel relief or experience sorrow at the loss of the baby. Although she wanted to give birth to Amar's child, she feared that Rohit would soon discover that he was not the father. And she dreaded the consequences of her husband learning the truth about the child.

#

As she was advised to take complete bed rest post the miscarriage, Nita did not venture out until she was fully recovered. And once she had recuperated well, Rohit wanted his wife to be a part of the official social circle.

"The Chairman is throwing a party at his residence, and I would like you to accompany me to the do like all other executive wives. And since you will be making your debut at the official event, I want you to make a good first impression," Rohit stated.

"And when is the party being held?" Nita asked.

"Well, it's next Sunday," Rohit replied.

"I've never been to one of these office parties before. And what is the dress code? Do you think I should wear a chiffon sari or a heavy silk Kanjeevaram? Which do you think is appropriate for the occasion?"

Nita asked her husband.

"You cannot be serious about wearing a sari to the party," Rohit said.

"Yes, of course," Nita affirmed. "And what's wrong with wearing a sari?" She asked. "I think it's very graceful."

"In Mercara, maybe, but not in Mumbai; Women in Mumbai are very westernized, and I expect you to wear a dress for the occasion," Rohit answered.

"I am afraid I don't have anything that's appropriate for a party, and I'll probably look a rag in what I possess," Nita averred.

"That's no problem as we could go shopping over the weekend. And I'll help you pick out a dress for the occasion," Rohit said.

Rohit accompanied Nita to the boutique that Saturday. There was an array of dresses on display at the shop. He briefly inspected the garments which were displayed on the rack before selecting a pastel pink one shoulder full length gown.

"Why don't you try this dress to see how it fits?" Rohit handed Nita the gown he had chosen.

Nita proceeded to the trial room before she emerged wearing the dress. The gown fit her perfectly, but the neckline, however, was a bit too deep as it showed a generous amount of her bosom.

"This neckline is rather plunging, and I feel practically naked in this dress. The low cut reveals too much cleavage, and I don't like exposing my breasts. And I'm not comfortable showing so much skin." Nita stated.

"Nonsense, you look fine. In fact, you will be very modest when compared to the other ladies. You should see what some of them wear." Rohit endeavored to allay his wife's fears.

"Are you sure that this dress is alright? And that I don't look vulgar in it?"

Nita asked Rohit.

"Yes, absolutely; you look just fine," Rohit reiterated.

#

They arrived at the CEO's residence at Malabar Hills shortly after 8.30 P.M. And when they showed up at the venue, they found that the other guests had reached before them, and that they were the last to arrive. There were around thirty couples at the do, and while the men were attired in Armani and Versace suits, their wives wore exclusive designer gowns. The expensive dresses had burned a considerable hole in their husbands' pockets as their wives were rather high maintenance. A few of the ladies were so extensively botoxed that their faces barely moved, and they appeared plastic in their desperate bid to cling to their fading youth.

Nita was the cynosure of many a male eye as Rohit proudly flaunted his wife. He was aware of the effect that she had on the other men in the room, and it was for this reason that he had chosen this particular dress for the occasion. The gown was revealing without seeming obscene, and Nita showed just the right amount of skin without appearing to be vulgar.

Rohit sought out their host shortly after they had arrived, and he greeted him.

"You haven't introduced me to your charming wife."

Their host stated.

"This is Ravi Pandit. He is the CEO."

Rohit made Nita's acquaintance with the Chief Executive Officer of the organization.

"Pleased to meet you," Nita stated, smiling shyly at Ravi. She was intimidated by her husband's boss, and she was rather unsure of how to conduct herself in his presence.

"You are now a part of this big family. Welcome to the fold." Ravi shook Nita's hand in greeting. He was aware of her discomfiture, and he tried to put her at ease.

Ravi's gaze followed Nita throughout the evening, and he found himself taking a keen interest in her. And he could not quite take his eyes off Rohit's wife.

Nita was extremely uncomfortable at the do, and she felt awkward and out of place as she did not quite fit in with the crowd. She was gauche next to the chic, sophisticated women, and she came across as a rustic.

#

It was well into the wee hours of the morning when the party finally wound up. And as some of the men were rather too drunk by that time to take the wheel; their chauffeurs would be driving them back home.

Rohit, however, was a social drinker who had nursed a glass through the evening, and he was sober enough to drive. His wife and he journeyed home in silence as they were each lost in their own thought. And the party was upper most on both their minds.

Nita had noticed Ravi Pandit follow her every move, and she was perturbed by his obvious attention. And she was embarrassed by the undue interest that her husband's boss had shown in her.

Rohit was pleased by the impression that Nita had made, and he realized that he was the envy of every male at the party. His wife was the most beautiful woman at the do, and all the other ladies had paled in comparison to her.

CHAPTER 6

Ravi Pandit had the dubious distinction of being a womanizer, and he was known to have a weakness for anything in a skirt. And it was his insatiable appetite for the fairer sex which had spelt the doom of his marriage. Ravi was a serial philanderer who flitted from one woman to another. And he had no qualms about cheating on his spouse since womanizing was second nature to him. His infidelity was the cause of much strife in the marriage, and when his wife caught him in bed with the baby sitter, that was the last straw. She walked out on him that very instant with their children in tow before filing for a divorce. And though his divorce cost him a small fortune, it was but a small price to pay when compared to the freedom that he now enjoyed. Ravi had the pleasure of bedding a different woman every night without being weighed down by the pangs of guilt.

He was now smitten with Nita, and she was constantly in his thoughts. Ravi was besotted by Rohit's wife, and he could not quite get her out of his head. Nita had a mesmerizing effect on him, and her naivety and innocence was intoxicating. He found her to be different from all the other women he had met, and he desired to have her.

He took his good friend and colleague, Rahul Deo, into confidence, and he confessed his interest in Nita to him. And he told Rahul that he was completely bowled over by Rohit's wife.

#

Rahul Deo and Ravi Pandit went back a long way. They had graduated from the Indian Institute of Technology, Powai, together before they set out to get a degree in Business Administration from the Indian Institute of Management, Ahmedabad. They subsequently joined Stan Express Bank as interns, and they gradually rose in the ranks. While Ravi went on to head the Organization as the Chief Executive Officer, Rahul became the second in command. And as the Managing Director, Rahul reported to The Chairman & Chief Executive Officer. While Rahul and Ravi remained mere colleagues at the work place, they were, however, thick as thieves outside of the office. And each was privy to the other's secrets as they hid nothing from each other. Even the sordid details of their respective sexual escapades were not spared, and each was aware of the other's carnal adventures.

"Rahul, I seem to have taken quite a fancy to Rohit's wife. And I cannot quite get her off my mind," Ravi said to Rahul.

"Well, that's nothing new anyways since I know you well enough not to expect it of you. And as I am well aware of your weakness for the fair sex, I'm not surprised that Nita has caught your eye," Rahul stated. He was not surprised to learn about Ravi's interest in Rohit's wife since he knew his friend well enough not to be shocked by him. He was well aware of Ravi's roving eye, and he was privy to his friend's philandering ways. Besides, Ravi had not told him anything that he had not heard before.

"And you know me. I'm not content with merely admiring a woman from afar, and would be interested in a carnal relationship with her. And I will not rest until I succeed in getting Nita into bed with me," Ravi stated.

"Well, that's nothing new either. And knowing you, I suppose you've already worked out a plan to worm your way into Nita's life," Rahul said.

"No, I'm afraid not, and that is the real tragedy here. And I am completely at a loss as to how to evoke Nita's interest since I don't have any means to gain access to her," Ravi replied.

"Well, it's pretty simple don't you think? I thought you would've already figured it out by now," Rahul stated.

"And what do you mean by that?" Ravi asked.

"Since the route to Nita is through her husband, you will have to deal with Rohit first before you succeed in getting to his wife," Rahul said.

"It's easier said than done. And how am I supposed to do that?" Ravi queried.

"For starters, you will need to get to know Rohit on a personal level. And by that I mean you should treat him more like a friend rather than a mere employee, and earn his trust. That's the only way you'll be able to worm your way into Nita's life," Rahul averred.

"That's a wonderful suggestion. And you are truly a genius since I couldn't have thought of it myself," Ravi replied.

"You're most welcome."

Rahul said dryly, as he acknowledged Ravi's appreciation.

"I didn't quite expect you to come up with such a brilliant idea," Ravi reiterated.

"You really do need to give me some credit here. After all, we've been friends long enough to know how your mind works." Rahul took offence at being undermined by Ravi.

#

Rohit Kumar was one of the youngest Vice-Presidents in the Organization, and Ravi was rather impressed with him. Ravi saw immense potential in Rohit, and he expected the latter to ascend in hierarchy until he reached the top. And he would not be surprised should Rohit reach the CEO's position, and occupy his chair some day.

Ravi had met Rohit a couple of times to discuss work but his official interaction with Rohit Kumar did not count for much. The meetings were usually very formal and only work related matters were discussed. They met either in the Conference Room or in Ravi's office and they were never ever alone. And the only communication between the two was either a polite smile or a brief word. Ravi now decided to extend the hand of friendship to his subordinate.

He buzzed for his secretary who entered his room in an instant. "Dahlia, tell Rohit Kumar that I wish to meet him right away," Ravi said.

"Yes, of course," Dahlia affirmed, before proceeding to convey Ravi's message to Rohit. She called him over the intercom and informed him that the CEO sought an immediate audience with him.

Rohit proceeded to the 24th floor to meet Ravi. And as he wend his way to Ravi's office, he wondered why the Chief Executive Officer wanted to see him. Since his financial report was long overdue, he hoped that he was not about to get a dressing-down and that he would not be reprimanded for his tardiness.

Once Rohit reached the CEO's office, Dahlia asked him to wait outside while she checked with Ravi.

It was Dahlia's job to screen all visitors who came to see Ravi, and no one was allowed to enter his room without her first ensuring that they had an appointment with him.

"Rohit Kumar is here to meet you."

Dahlia informed Ravi.

"Please send him in." Ravi granted his secretary permission to usher Rohit into his room.

"Mr. Pandit will see you now."

Dahlia addressed Rohit.

"May I come in, Sir?"

Rohit sought Ravi's permission before entering.

"Yes, of course, please do."

Ravi gestured to Rohit to take a seat. Even before Rohit could pull up a chair and sit down, Ravi asked for coffee.

"By the way Dahlia, could I request you to send in two cups of Espresso?"

"Yes, of course, Mr. Pandit," Dahlia affirmed, before leaving the room to comply with Ravi's request.

As Rohit sat speculating about the purpose of the meeting, Ravi's private line rang. Ravi answered the phone briefly before disconnecting the call. He then turned to address Rohit.

"You probably must be wondering why I wanted to see you," Ravi stated.

"Yes, that's right," Rohit answered.

"Well, you can rest assured that it's got nothing to do with work. I thought that it would be a good idea to get to know my staff on a more personal level. I understand that you are recently married."

"Yes, that's right," Rohit replied.

"And how does your wife like Mumbai as I'm told that she is from a small town?" Ravi asked Rohit. "The metropolitan can be quite intimidating for a small Towner."

"Well, Nita did find it difficult initially to live in a bustling city, and she was a bit homesick at first. But then, she seems to have adjusted quite well. Mumbai is a city that tends to grow on you. I think she rather likes it here now, and she is gradually turning into the typical Mumbaikar," Rohit answered.

"I'm glad to hear that your family life is fine as your performance at the work place tends to get affected should there be any tensions at home. And should you be unhappy for some reason, you will be unable to give your one hundred percent to the job. I must mention here that Rahul is pretty impressed with you, and he speaks rather highly of you," Ravi said.

As Rohit reported to the Managing Director, Rahul Deo had done his employee evaluation. And Rohit was given an excellent appraisal by his boss.

"I try to do my best." Rohit graciously accepted Ravi's compliment. He endeavored to be modest while acknowledging the CEO's appreciation since he did not want to appear to be pompous and arrogant. And even though Ravi was being cordial, Rohit ensured that he did not overstep his bounds with the CEO.

"Well, I will be seeing you at the Executives' Meeting scheduled for later today at the Conference Room. You do know that I am presiding over the meet." Ravi reminded Rohit about the executives' meeting that was scheduled to be held after lunch. "And that will be all." He dismissed Rohit from his room.

Ravi ensured that he was kept well informed about Rohit. And everything that Rohit did was privy to the Chief Executive Officer.

#

Rohit tried to focus on the camera while his tongue snaked along the man's naked body. And as he meandered along the hairy terrain, the man's body heaved with pleasure. Rohit's tongue travelled from the man's mouth to the neck and along his belly before resting on his erogenous zone. And as Rohit stimulated him, the man's low moan reached a crescendo before he exploded in Rohit's mouth.

"Please don't stop," the man begged.

Rohit spat out the man's discharge, and he rinsed his mouth in the sink, before resuming the erotic play. The man was an animal whose sexual appetite was insatiable. Rohit would be required to pleasure him over and over again until the first streak of light appeared in the sky. And it would be one hell of a long, exhausting night.

CHAPTER 7

Rohit was promoted as Senior Vice-President – Finance, following the exit of his predecessor from the organization, and he was one of the youngest to be appointed to the post in the history of Stan Express Bank. Rohit's promotion, however, did not go down too well with many in the organization as there were others in the fray who were senior to him, and they felt that they deserved to get the promotion rather than him. And they reckoned that the post of Senior VP should have been theirs. Rohit's senior colleagues were offended when they were overlooked for the position which was awarded to a junior instead. And there were murmurs of discontent amongst the disgruntled.

Rohit's mercurial rise in the organization set tongues wagging, and malicious rumours began doing the rounds since his colleagues cast aspersions upon him. And though they lacked the courage to confront him in person, there were, however, many seedy whisperings behind his back.

"I'm sure Gita recommended Rohit Kumar for the promotion when the post fell vacant following Pramod's resignation," his colleagues stated.

Rahul's wife Gita, invariably singled out Rohit at office parties by showing special interest in him, and she went to great lengths to bestow her attention upon him. It was pretty evident that she was rather fond of Rohit, and some were even convinced that the two were having a clandestine affair. As Gita wielded considerable influence over her husband, Rohit's out of turn promotion was attributed to the Managing Director's wife. And she was rumoured to be instrumental for his recent elevation.

Raveena was the secretary to the Senior Vice-President, and she was entrusted with the job of handling his schedules at the office. And those who wished to seek an appointment with Rohit were required to approach Raveena before they were granted an audience with him.

#

A meeting was scheduled at the Conference Room for late in the afternoon. Rohit was busy working on his presentation for the occasion when his head began to throb. Reading the signals of the onset of a migraine, he immediately took a pill. Rohit swallowed an aspirin along with a hot cup of coffee. And when he arrived at the Conference Room for the meeting, his headache had long subsided, and he felt fine.

The meet was chaired by the CEO, and it was pretty late when the discussions finally concluded. And as they were all rather hungry by then, they were served tea and biscuits before they left for the day.

Ravi turned to Rohit, and he addressed him. "I'd like to see you in my office before you leave," he said.

"Yes, of course," Rohit replied.

#

Rohit proceeded to Ravi's office soon after the meeting. He was shown into the CEO's room by his secretary, Dahlia. Although it was rather late in the evening, Dahlia, however, was still at work since she seldom left before Ravi.

"I hope I'm not keeping you from doing anything important? And I hope you are not inconvenienced by staying back after work?"

Ravi asked Rohit.

"No, not at all," Rohit replied.

"Are you free tonight? Or do you have any plans for the night? Is there any prior engagement that I'm keeping you from?" Ravi asked.

"No, I have no particular plans for tonight," Rohit stated. And should he have any plans for the evening, he would be willing to cancel everything in a bid to oblige Ravi.

"Good. Then would you like to join me for a couple of drinks at the bar?" Ravi asked Rohit. "I could do with the company tonight."

"Yes, of course, if that's alright with you."

Rohit accepted Ravi's invitation, and he agreed to spend the evening with him in spite of having other plans for the night. He had promised to take Nita to watch the new play which had opened at the NCPA, and she would be waiting for him. Rohit, however, chose not to inform his wife about the change in plans, and he hoped to come up with a convincing explanation once he reached home later that night.

#

Ravi took Rohit to a pub on Marine Drive. The place was filled to capacity with a Friday evening crowd whose weekend had already begun. The patrons were waited upon by stylishly attired cocktail waitresses who took their order.

"What would you like to have?"

Ravi asked Rohit.

"Well, I'm not much of a drinker and would prefer to have beer," Rohit replied.

"Well then, I shall order beer for both of us. Would you prefer Lager or Stout?" Ravi asked.

"Lager would be fine," Rohit replied.

Ravi gestured to the waitress. "We'd like to order beer. I'll have Stout while my friend here will have Lager." He placed the order on behalf of the both of them.

The waitress arrived shortly with their drinks.

Rohit went slow with the beer, and he settled for a mug through the evening.

Ravi, on the other hand, was rather generous with the ale, and he downed a couple of mugs of beer in quick succession. And though he was a tad tipsy after the feat, Ravi, however, conducted himself well, and he gave no cause for any embarrassment.

"Today is a sad day for me," Ravi said; attempting to start a conversation.

"How so?" Rohit asked.

"Today is my parents' death anniversary, and I lost them both on this day," Ravi replied.

"I am really sorry to hear that." Rohit sympathized with Ravi when he heard that his parents were no more.

"I hate to be alone on this day as it revives bitter memories of the day I lost them." Ravi reiterated. "And that's the reason why I was desperate for company tonight."

"I can understand how you feel, and I'm sure you must get very lonely at times as parents are our support system," Rohit said.

"I had a terrible fight with my parents on the day that they died. And I never got the chance to tell them how sorry I was," Ravi rued.

"I can imagine how hard that must be for you, and it's probably still weighing on your conscience. Would it help to talk about it?" Rohit offered to lend Ravi a sympathetic ear.

"My parents were killed in an air accident, and as the wreckage of the plane was never found, the aircraft was presumed to have crashed into the ocean. I had a huge showdown with them that morning as my brother and I were not allowed to accompany them on account of our annual exams. And that's the last memory I have of them."

"And that must be really terrible."

"Yes, it is indeed."

"Have you made your peace with it?"

Rohit asked Ravi.

"Well, I was angry with God for a long time for being cruel to take my parents away while I still needed them, but then I gradually learned to make my peace with it. However, every year on this day the bitter memories come back, and I make a conscious effort never to be alone as I feel absolutely miserable," Ravi averred.

"And how old were you when you lost your parents?"

Rohit asked Ravi.

"I was barely twelve and my brother was nine when our parents died."

"And who raised you after your parents passed away?"

Rohit asked Ravi.

"We were brought up by our maternal grandmother after our parents were gone," Ravi said.

"I'm sure your grandmother must be pretty old now. Does she live with your brother?" Rohit queried.

"She passed away a long time ago, and God bless her soul. Our grandmother was a strong woman who remained brave for our sakes. I never once saw her grieve for her daughter in our presence; and I'm sure she must have felt her loss. That's the kind of woman she was," Ravi replied.

Rohit caught a glimpse of Ravi's vulnerability tonight. He was unlike the intimidating organizational head with a stiff upper lip who maintained his distance with the staff. Rohit realized that despite the tough image that the CEO portrayed, he was susceptible to both pain and sorrow.

They sat talking until late into the night, and before they knew it, the clock had struck twelve.

"I didn't quite realize that it was midnight already. Time seems to have flown by." Ravi remarked, when he heard the clock strike the witching hour.

"I think we should go home now. My wife will probably be worried sick wondering where I am as I didn't inform her that I'd be late," Rohit stated.

"I'm rather hungry and hate to go home to a cold dinner as my cook has taken the day off," Ravi said. "Why don't you join me for a quick bite?" He asked.

"Alright," Rohit replied.

"I know a Punjabi restaurant just round the corner that is an all night joint. Their service is quick and the food is good too," Ravi said.

They exited from the pub and proceeded to the restaurant.

#

Punjabi Darbar was a family owned restaurant situated at Churchgate, and the eatery was run by a middle-aged couple. A huge statue of the Hindu Elephant God, Lord

Ganesha, stood at the entrance to the restaurant, whilst strains of the Sitar floated in the background. The staff was attired in traditional Pathani suit complete with turbaned headgear and white gloves. The husband and wife team greeted the diners at the door before they were escorted to the table.

Ravi summoned a waiter once they were seated. "We'll have chicken biryani and mutton curry along with sheekh kebab and chicken tikka, and of course, the famous Punjabi lassi. And could you make it quick please as we are in a bit of a hurry." He instructed, whilst placing their order.

"Yes, of course," the waiter affirmed.

Their food arrived shortly. While the meal was sumptuous, it was rather spicy with more than a generous dash of chillies.

Rohit found the fare a bit too pungent for his liking, while Ravi, on the other hand, relished the meal.

"I'm picking up the tab and there will be no arguments." Ravi insisted on paying the bill. He brought out his VISA Debit Card from his wallet and settled the tariff before they stepped out of the eatery.

#

Rohit expected to have a show down with Nita when he returned home, and he braced himself for a war of words with his wife. Nita, however, was asleep when he arrived at the apartment, and the evening passed by without any ugly incident.

CHAPTER 8

Rao Bahadur had grown rather old, and he was now in the twilight of his life. And as he had aged considerably, his faculties were gradually beginning to diminish. He was now hard of hearing as he had turned practically deaf in one ear and was loath to wear a hearing aid. And he was not as agile as before since he now moved about with the aid of a walking stick in spite of which his gait was not quite steady, and he tottered with each step that he took. His vision, however, was still very sharp, and despite his advanced years, Rao Bahadur was as sharp sighted as an eagle.

Most of his contemporaries were long dead, and their passing was mentioned in the obituary column of the local newspaper. And every time he read about the news of some one's demise, he realized that he was now close to death. He knew that it was only a matter of time before he too passed away and featured in the obituaries.

Rao Bahadur's Will was already executed, and he was bequeathing his entire estate to his daughter. Nita would be sole heiress to the plantation, and she would be the mistress of the manor, while Ganga would be allowed to remain until her death. Since Rao Bahadur did not want Ganga to worry about her future after he was gone, he ensured that she would be well cared for until the end. As Ganga had remained loyal to the family all these years, he felt that it was the least that he could do for the woman who had devoted her entire life to raising his motherless daughter.

#

Rao Bahadur had just finished having his evening tea when Dr. Amit arrived. Dr. Amit was Dr. Gowda's son who had taken over his father's practice after his death. And most of Dr. Gowda's former patients were now being treated by his son. Dr. Amit had stopped by to check on Rao Bahadur to see how he was doing. As the latter seldom left the manor now-a-days, and he was more or less confined to his home, Dr. Amit made house calls to monitor his elderly patient's health. And the doctor came by regularly to examine Rao Bahadur.

"How are you feeling now?"

Dr. Amit asked Rao Bahadur.

"As well as anyone my age can."

Rao Bahadur quipped.

Dr. Amit proceeded to examine Rao Bahadur. He checked his patient's blood pressure and his blood sugar, and he listened to the rhythm of Rao Bahadur's heart beat before writing out a prescription. "Now, do remember to take your medicines on time, and don't slip up on your medication." Dr. Amit instructed Rao Bahadur.

As Rao Bahadur had turned senile with age, he forgot more than he remembered. And there were many a time when he skipped his medication since he did not remember to take his pills.

Dr. Amit turned to Ganga after he had examined Rao Bahadur. "I wish to speak to you in private," he said. "Can we step outside for a minute?" He asked.

"Yes, of course," Ganga affirmed.

They stepped out of Rao Bahadur's room before Dr. Amit addressed Ganga. "Now that we are out of your master's earshot, I'm going to very honest with you. I am afraid that my patient's health is failing, and I fear that he'll be gone soon." Dr. Amit said.

"Well, I'm not surprised to hear that. And that was bound to happen anyways," Ganga stated.

"And what do you mean by that?" Dr. Amit asked.

"There's something that I've to tell you, but the master should never know that you heard it from me. You have to promise that you will not betray my confidence," Ganga said.

"You can rest assured that I won't breathe a word to anyone, and I'll remain mum. In fact, your master will never learn of this conversation." Dr. Amit promised Ganga that he would not repeat what he heard.

"Well, if you must know, master is not regular in taking his medicines. And I don't know whether it's deliberate, or whether he's just being forgetful and absent-minded," Ganga said.

"Are you quite certain?" Dr. Amit asked Ganga. He had his reservations about Rao Bahadur's medication as there was no improvement in his patient's condition. Rather the latter's health was gradually deteriorating, and he was frailer each time that Dr. Amit checked on him. And the doctor feared that his elderly patient would not be alive when he wished to see the latter next.

"I've seen the master throw the pills away. And it seems like he doesn't want to get any better," Ganga said.

"I don't understand why he does not wish to take care of his health. Rao Bahadur doesn't come across as a man who does not want to live," Dr. Amit said, when he learned that his patient was flushing the prescription pills down the toilet.

"Perhaps, it's his daughter."

Ganga muttered under her breath.

Dr. Amit heard Ganga despite the undertone. "Well, what about Nita?" He asked. "I was under the impression that she was happily married, and that she was well settled with her husband."

"Nothing, and forget that I even mentioned her." Ganga realized that she had revealed much more than she had intended to, and she decided to hold her tongue before it was too late. Since the master trusted her to protect the secrets of the manor; she did not want to betray him by exposing the skeletons in the family cupboard.

#

Ganga was worried after her conversation with Dr. Amit, and she was perturbed by what she had been told. The doctor had hinted that her master would not live for much longer, and she wanted to confront him about the sordid past before it was too late. And though she was well aware that she was crossing the line, she, however, had no other option. Should she go to her grave without the truth being told, she would never rest in peace.

She sought out Rao Bahadur after dinner, and she found the master in the study. She knocked gently on the study door before entering the room. "I'm sorry to disturb you, but I need to speak with you urgently." She apologized to Rao Bahadur for intruding upon his private time.

Rao Bahadur usually did a bit of reading in the study before he retired for the night, and it was a habit that he had cultivated since Nita had left the manor.

"That's quite alright. I was getting ready to retire for the night anyway." Rao Bahadur said. He closed the book and laid it upon the table, before removing his reading glasses and placing it in the case.

"Master, I do realize that I'm only a servant. And I hope you don't feel that I'm stepping out of bounds. But then don't you think that it's time you told Nita the truth?"

Ganga addressed Rao Bahadur rather hesitantly since she did not want to come across as being impudent as that was not her place. And though the master treated her like family, she never ever forgot the fact that she was only an employee, and that she was not expected to breach that position. Although she was apprehensive of Rao Bahadur's response, she was, however, prepared to face her master's wrath. And she was willing to bear the brunt of his ire for Nita's sake, since she owed it to the latter to let her know the truth.

Rao Bahadur never forgave himself for betraying Nita as he felt that he had done grave injustice to his daughter. And he was ridden with guilt ever since. His treachery weighed heavily upon his conscience, and he had spent many sleepless nights repenting for the unpardonable act that he had committed. He was blinded by rage at the time, and he had failed to consider the consequences of his actions. And by the time realization dawned upon him, it was too late to make amends. "As a matter of fact, I've been thinking of the same thing myself. I'm going to call Nita first thing tomorrow morning and confess everything to her since I need to get this load off my chest before my lips are sealed forever," he said. His tone was suspiciously gruff, and his eyes were moist. And he was having a hard time trying to keep his tears in check.

CHAPTER 9

Nita had her head buried in the closet, and she was trying to pick out a dress from her wardrobe when she heard the sound of the telephone ringing. Her father called her regularly to enquire about her welfare, and he telephoned her every once in a while to find out how she was doing. And Nita always looked forward to speaking to him. However, when she answered the telephone, she heard Ganga's voice at the other end.

"Hello, Ganga, I didn't quite expect it to be you on the line." Nita said. "Where's papa?" She asked her nanny.

Ganga did not answer immediately. And she paused briefly before replying to Nita. "I'm afraid I've some terrible news to convey to you," she said.

"Well, just how bad is it?" Nita queried.

"It's about your father. I called to tell you that your father has passed away. And that he is no more," Ganga said.

"The last time I spoke to papa he sounded pretty sick, but I didn't quite expect him to die so soon," Nita said.

"Well, your father's death was very sudden."

"And how so?" Nita asked.

"The master slipped into a coma post a bad fall and he died soon thereafter," Ganga replied.

"And I suppose you're waiting for me to arrive before papa's funeral can be held," Nita stated.

"I am afraid it's too late for that now. Your father passed away a week ago, and as the telephone lines were all down on account of the incessant rains, I couldn't inform you earlier. Master's body was kept in the morgue for a couple of days before we decided to go ahead with the funeral without waiting for you to arrive."

"And whose decision was it to go ahead with papa's funeral in spite of my not being present on the occasion?"

Nita asked Ganga.

"Dr. Amit took the decision to bury your father since his body was showing signs of decomposing, and he didn't want to wait any longer," Ganga answered.

"I would've liked to see papa one last time before he was buried, and I'm really upset with the turn of events. But then I suppose Dr. Amit took the right decision given the circumstances," Nita said. "Was there a large crowd at papa's funeral considering that he was very well known in the town?" She asked.

"Your father was buried on the grounds of the estate, and he was laid to rest next to your mother. The funeral was a very private affair with only the household staff in attendance. And Dr. Amit was the lone outsider who was present on the occasion," Ganga said.

"And has papa's passing been notified in the local newspapers so that people are aware that he is no more?" Nita asked.

"Yes, the local newspapers carried the news of your father's death, and his passing was announced in the obituaries. In fact, the manor has been receiving condolences since the announcement of his demise," Ganga replied.

"And what about the affairs of the estate, has that been taken care of?"

"The master took care of everything before he passed away. Your father's solicitor has been appointed the caretaker of the property, and he will look after the affairs of the estate until the time you decide to take charge," Ganga answered.

"It's good that the legalities are all taken care of. Or else it could lead to unnecessary complications," Nita stated.

"There's something else that I need to tell you besides the news of your father's passing. But, you must first promise that you won't hate your father and only then will I proceed."

"Well, papa is dead isn't he? So, I couldn't hurt him even if I wanted to," Nita replied.

"That's beside the point. Unless you give me your word that you won't bear any ill will towards the master, I refuse to proceed any further," Ganga reiterated.

"Alright, I promise I won't be mad at papa. And I hope you're happy to hear that."

"Before I begin, I must tell you that your father wanted to tell you this himself, but then he died before that. The day master decided to confess everything to you, he was rushed to the hospital, and he never recovered. Your father slipped into a coma as a result of a fall he had that morning, and he died soon thereafter. Even though master is dead, I speak for him. And I'm doing this on his behalf."

"Alright, I'm listening. Go on." Nita prompted Ganga, and she wondered what could be so terrible that she would end up loathing her father.

"It's regarding Amar…" Ganga said; and she was hesitant to speak about Rao Bahadur's bête noire.

"Well, what about Amar? And that was a long time ago anyway. Why are you raking up that topic after all these years?"

Nita asked Ganga.

"That's because Amar never walked out on you as you believed, but he was banished from your life," Ganga replied.

"What do you mean by saying that Amar was banished?"

Nita asked Ganga.

"That night after Amar returned from Bangalore, he met your father and he confessed to the master of his love for you. And he also mentioned to master that you were expecting his child, and he told your father that he wished to marry you. Your father flew into a rage when he learned that Amar was cozying up to you behind his back. You were born to be a mistress whereas Amar was a lowly hired hand, and he couldn't bear the thought of his supervisor romancing his daughter. Your father brought out his rifle to shoot Amar dead, and had I not intervened in time, the master would probably have killed him. And I had a difficult time trying to restrain the master. It took a lot of effort on my part to convince your father not to let his rage get the better of him since murder was the last thing he needed to have on his hands.

"Amar was told to leave the premises that very night. And your father personally arranged for the transport to take Amar to Bangalore since he did not want the latter on his property any longer. Although I was not very fond of Amar and didn't think much of him; all the same I felt sorry for him at the time. He was a completely broken man, and I saw him fall apart at being told to disappear from your life."

"At least now I know that Amar did not renege on his promise," Nita said when she was told that he was banished from her life by her father. "And is that all?" she asked.

"No, there's more."

"Alright, continue."

"Amar wrote several letters to you after he had left, and a letter arrived almost every day."

"Then why were the letters not given to me?" Nita asked.

"That's because the master had left strict instructions to hand over to him all letters that were addressed to you as he had a suspicion that Amar would resort to writing to you. And no one dared to disobey him as they feared they would lose their job," Ganga answered.

"Was my pregnancy the reason why papa got me married in such a hurry?" Nita queried.

"Yes, that's right. Your marriage was hastily fixed because of the condition you were in since your father couldn't risk your pregnancy becoming public. It would have brought shame and disgrace to the family, besides tarnishing his name. And you are well aware how deeply your father cared about his reputation. Your pregnancy was the reason your father got you married to someone who lived in Mumbai and not on an estate in Coorg as no one would know when the child was born. It would've caused quite a scandal if it was discovered that you had given birth in less than nine months after you were wed."

"Papa had an agenda in breaking my heart. But you at least could have been honest with me. I hold you guilty of hiding the truth from me, and I blame you for keeping me in the dark about the reason for Amar's disappearance," Nita said.

"And believe me, I did want to be honest with you, but I was not at liberty to tell you the truth since master had forbidden me from disclosing anything to you. And although I felt terribly guilty for lying, I was, however, left with no other choice since I couldn't risk invoking your father's ire by defying his diktat. Before you turn to hate your father, you should know that he regretted everything that he did. Master never forgave himself for breaking your heart, and he went to his grave with the guilt weighing heavily upon his conscience," Ganga concluded.

"Well, I'm glad that papa finally realized he had wronged me even though his remorse was too late. And it doesn't set things right anyway," Nita averred.

"Well, I've done my duty towards the master by telling you the truth. And, now I want you to keep your word about not holding any grudge against your father." Ganga held Nita to her promise.

"Alright, I promise I won't hate papa even after everything that I've learned."

Nita ended the call on that note. And when she hung up the telephone, she was shaking like a leaf, and she was trembling with pent-up emotion. She had remained composed during her conversation with Ganga, but she could no longer hold her tears in check. Nita broke down and wept inconsolably, and her torrent of tears did not stop flowing. Her father had led her to believe that Amar had betrayed her by walking out on her and their unborn child, and she had assumed that he had vanished from her life without so much as a trace. Nita had hated Amar all these years for betraying her trust, and she had loathed him for reneging on his promise. She now realized that Amar was as much a victim as she was while the villain turned out to be her father.

CHAPTER 10

Rohit was busy working at his laptop when his e-mail pinged, and he was notified about a recent mail that was received in his in-box. He stopped what he was doing at once, and he proceeded to read the new mail in order to ascertain its importance and urgency. He was, however, in for a rude shock when he read the contents of the mail. The e-mail was neither official nor was it important. Rather, the mail had been sent to him anonymously, and the content was smutty as it was filled with innuendos.

"I am aware of the lengths to which you have stooped to claw your way up the corporate ladder, and I know the abysmal depths to which you have sunk to rise in hierarchy. And you should hang your head in shame at the modus operandi adopted by you to pave your way to the top," the e-mail read.

Rohit was well aware of the seedy whisperings that was going around the work place, and he knew what was being said about him behind his back. The nasty rumours which were floating about him in the office had reached him as well, and he had no illusions about the impression that his fellow co-workers had about him. Rohit, however, chose to ignore the office gossip, and he had paid no heed to the malicious rumours about him, as he was not the first to fall a victim to jealous colleagues at the work place, and neither would he be the last. And since professional jealously existed in every organization; he remained unaffected by his colleagues' pettiness.

He, however, felt that sending an obscene mail was taking things a bit too far, and he reckoned that the nastiness was getting out of hand. And he mulled bringing the smutty e-mail to Ravi's attention before he thought the better of it. It would be rather silly on his part to bring such a trivial incident to the attention of the CEO when there were more pressing issues to be dealt with in the office. Since he did not wish to give undue importance to a mail that was of little consequence; he dismissed the smutty e-mail as the sick prank of a depraved mind. And Rohit deleted the offensive mail without giving any further thought to it.

A letter arrived for Rohit in the mail the following morning, and it was delivered to him at the office. There was nothing strange about a letter being delivered to him at the work place, except that it was marked "Private and Confidential." And since it stated that the cover had to be opened by the addressee only and no one else besides him, Raveena had left the letter unopened on Rohit's desk.

Rohit blanched when he opened the cover, and the colour drained from his face when he perceived the text. And he turned pale and ashen upon seeing the contents of the letter. The short, crisp letter was rather ominous, and he wondered how his closely guarded secret was discovered when no one was privy to it.

"I know what you are and I will tell. And the world shall soon learn of your shameful secret," the letter read.

Rohit was deeply disturbed by the anonymous letter and he was not in a proper frame of mind to conduct the post lunch meet that he was supposed to chair. And, as such, he decided to defer the discussions to the following day.

He buzzed for his secretary.

"Raveena, I'd like to postpone the meeting that was scheduled for this afternoon to the same time tomorrow. Could you please inform everyone about the change, and also apologize to them for the inconvenience caused by this last minute announcement?" Rohit instructed his secretary. "And do it right away," he added.

"Yes, of course," Raveena affirmed.

"Good and I certainly appreciate it."

"Are you alright?" Raveena asked Rohit. "You look rather perturbed."

"It's nothing, I'm fine," Rohit stated; choosing to lie to Raveena since he did not wish to pour out his troubles to her.

"Can I get you a strong cup of coffee?" Raveena asked. "Perhaps, that would help."

"Sounds like a good idea. And coffee would be just fine," Rohit said.

Rohit was summoned by the CEO later in the day for an important meeting. He found it difficult to pay attention while his mind was in an utter turmoil. And even as he sat through the discussion, it was a herculean effort for him to remain focused. "Are you alright?" Ravi asked Rohit. "You seem rather distracted today," he remarked.

"It's nothing. I guess I lost focus," Rohit replied.

A parcel arrived by courier for Rohit a few days later, and the package was delivered to him at his work place. The parcel contained a couple of private photographs that were meant for his eyes only. As Rohit had personally borne witness to these photographs being destroyed, he was at a loss to understand how these snapshots had managed to surface in spite of them having been obliterated. And he wondered how the photographs had fallen into the hands of a complete stranger when they no longer existed.

Since he could not risk taking the raunchy snapshots home; Rohit kept the photographs in the safe at the office where they would be well hidden from prying eyes. As he was the only one who had access to the office safe, no one else apart from him would lay their hands on these intimate photographs. Rohit wished to destroy the raunchy pictures once he reached office the next day, and he wanted to wipe out all traces of the racy snapshots. However, when he arrived at the office the following morning, Rohit was dismayed to discover that the photographs were missing. The telltale pictures had vanished, and they had disappeared from the safe.

#

"I couldn't help noticing that you've been rather off colour of late. Is everything alright with you?"

Ravi asked Rohit one morning.

"Yes, all's well," Rohit replied.

"You've been working far too hard lately and it's time you took a break. I will be kind enough to give you a week off since you need the vacation. And I want you to relax and enjoy yourself, and forget about work. I've a friend who owns a beach house in Alibaug and I'll arrange for you to holiday there. It wouldn't be such a bad idea for you to take a couple of days off and get away with your wife to enjoy the sun and the surf. I'm sure the change will do you both good," Ravi said.

"Well, I'd like to go on a vacation as it's been nothing but work lately. And I could really do with the break. But then, are you quite sure that you can afford to let me go?"

Rohit asked Ravi.

"It's only a week, for crying out loud. And the heavens certainly won't fall down while you are away," Ravi shrugged.

CHAPTER 11

Rohit was over an hour late getting to work this morning as he had to stop by at the ATM to withdraw money. And the serpentine queue outside the automated teller machine had led to this inordinate delay. He had barely settled down at his desk at the office when he received an internal call from Ravi's secretary.

"Mr. Pandit would like to see you immediately. Could you please proceed to his office right away?" Dahlia stated over the telephone.

Rohit left his office soon after receiving Dahlia's call to proceed to see the CEO. And when he passed Rahul's room, he stepped inside to have a word with him. Rahul, however, was not in his office as he was yet to arrive for the day, and that was quite unusual since he was generally one of the first to be at work. As it was rather unlike Rahul to be late for the office, Rohit couldn't help wondering whether Gita had taken a sudden turn for the worse.

Rahul's wife was ailing for some time now, and she was under care at home with a full-time nurse to tend to her. And though she was recovering quite well, the doctors, however, had not ruled out the possibility of a sudden relapse that could result in hospitalization.

When Rohit reached Ravi's office, Dahlia did not greet him with her usual friendly smile. But she was rather terse and brusque, and she looked very grim. And neither did she take the trouble to usher Rohit into the CEO's office; like she normally did.

Rohit let himself inside Ravi's room before greeting him. "Good morning Sir, may I come in?" He sought the CEO's permission to take his seat.

Ravi acknowledged Rohit's greeting with a brief nod but the customary hello was not forthcoming. And he did not attempt to be friendly and affable. Ravi looked haggard and drawn, and there were purple shadows under his eyes which was a telltale sign of a sleepless night. Besides; he was carelessly attired as his clothes were a tad creased, and his tie was loosely knotted. And he did not appear to have taken the trouble to shave before arriving at the office this morning, as the stubble was clearly visible on his face.

Rohit was taken aback by Ravi's disheveled appearance as he did not quite expect the CEO to turn up at the office in this shabby manner. As Ravi was usually very suave and dapper, and he was well groomed to the hilt, Rohit figured that something was terribly amiss for the CEO to have put in an appearance at work sporting a bedraggled look.

Ravi proceeded to address Rohit. And even as he attempted to speak, he appeared to be struggling for words.

"I'm afraid I've some terrible news. Rahul Deo is no more. He passed away last night," Ravi said. And as he made that announcement, he was having a hard time trying to keep his emotions in check, and he was finding it difficult not to breakdown. As Rahul and Ravi were rather close, losing Rahul was akin to the loss of a beloved member of the family. And Ravi was mourning the passing of a dear friend who was more like a brother to him.

"I am really sorry to hear about Rahul's passing. That is terrible indeed. And how did he die since it's all very sudden?" Rohit asked. He was shocked to know that Rahul had passed away, and he could not quite believe that the latter was gone. The Managing Director's death was very sudden, and he found it difficult to accept that he was no more. Rohit found it hard to come to terms with the fact that he would never see Rahul again.

"Gita and he were having a heated argument over some issue, and things got so completely out of hand that it ended with her shooting Rahul dead before she turned the gun upon herself. And when the housekeeper heard the commotion, she tried to stop them, but even before she could intervene in their quarrel, it was all over and they were both dead. Sapna called me immediately after the incident, and she was in such great shock that she didn't quite know what to do. I rushed to Rahul's place soon after I got her call. And I informed the police while I was on my way to his apartment, before notifying the family of the tragedy."

"I fail to understand how it could have happened. Isn't Gita under the care of a full-time nurse? And wasn't she around at the time?" Rohit asked.

"Since Gita was making progress, she dispensed with the service of the nurse. And she was able to take care of herself," Ravi replied.

"Anyways, it's a terrible tragedy. And it should never have happened," Rohit stated.

"I will make a formal announcement about Rahul's death later in the day. But meanwhile, I'd like you to keep this information to yourself," Ravi said.

"Yes, of course, I understand," Rohit averred. "I will leave it to you to let the rest of the organization know about Rahul."

#

The Senior Executives were asked to assemble in the Conference Room later in the day.

"I have hastily convened this meeting to inform you of the passing away of a Senior Member of our Team. Our Managing Director, Rahul Deo, is no more as he died last night."

Ravi announced the death of Rahul Deo at the Executives' gathering. And he broke the tragic news of the Managing Director's untimely demise sans providing the details that had led to his passing. Ravi left the Conference Room soon after making that announcement without having any further discussion on the subject.

A hushed silence befell the shocked audience following Ravi's announcement, and they were all very somber as they were grief stricken. They were saddened to learn of the Managing Director's sudden passing, and they were struggling to come to terms with the terrible tragedy. However, even on that solemn occasion there was much speculation since they could not help wondering who Rahul Deo's successor would be.

CHAPTER 12

Tanmay Beri took over as the Managing Director following Rahul's demise. He had joined Stan Express Bank as a Management Trainee, and he had gradually risen in the organization. And his dedication and hard work saw him swiftly climb the corporate ladder, and ascend in hierarchy. Tanmay was a confirmed bachelor who declared that he had no need for a wife since he was already married to his job.

The position of Executive Vice-President fell vacant following Tanmay's promotion, and there were many contenders for the post. However, much to everyone's surprise, the coveted post went to Rohit Kumar. And Rohit was soon promoted as the Executive Vice-President of Stan Express Bank.

Tanmay's secretary, Rina, resigned soon after his promotion as she would no longer be working for the organization. Rina quit her job to be a homemaker since she wished to devote her time to raising her children. Subsequent to Rina's resignation, Raveena took her place, and she would be working as secretary to the Executive Vice-President from now onwards.

Rohit's career graph was now on the rise and Lady Luck was smiling down upon him. He had achieved considerable success in a relatively short span of time, and he had swiftly ascended the corporate ladder. And it would not be long before he reached the top. Rohit hoped to retire as The Chairman & Chief Executive Officer of Stan Express Bank some day.

#

Rohit and Ravi often had their meals together at the executives' dining room. And they usually sat at the same table for lunch.

"By the way, what are you doing tonight? Do you have any plans for the night?"

Ravi asked Rohit over lunch one afternoon.

"Well, I promised to take Nita out to dinner tonight and the reservations have already been made. And as we are a large group, it is rather difficult to cancel at the last minute since everyone has to be informed," Rohit replied.

"That's a real shame as I was hoping you'd be able to come over to my place for dinner tonight. And I had looked forward to our time together. Anyways what about tomorrow night? And don't disappoint me again by telling me that you have plans for tomorrow as well," Ravi said.

"Tomorrow should be fine as we have nothing planned for the night," Rohit stated.

"Okay, that's great, then how about you and your wife join me for dinner tomorrow night?" Ravi asked Amar. "And I won't take 'no' for an answer this time. My daughter will be there too as she is down for the weekend. And you will get to meet her."

"Yes, we'd like that very much, thank you," Rohit affirmed. He accepted Ravi's dinner invitation on behalf of both Nita and himself. So far as he was aware, his wife had no plans for tomorrow night and she would be free to attend the dinner at Ravi's apartment. And should she have any engagement for the evening, Rohit would ask her to postpone the same to a later date. As Ravi was the most important person in their life at present, he had precedence over everything else. And Rohit did not want to displease him by declining his invitation.

"Since I eat early, I'd like you to be there by 8 o'clock. And I will be expecting you to show up with your wife." Ravi confirmed dinner at his apartment the following night.

#

Rohit and his wife reached Ravi's apartment just as the clock struck 8 o'clock. They were met at the door by the butler who showed them inside. And they were led to the lounge where their host was awaiting the arrival of his guests.

"I'm glad you could make it tonight." Ravi greeted his guests warmly. He was delighted to meet Nita again, and he could not quite conceal his pleasure at seeing her. Even though Nita was modestly attired in a high necked full length dress that covered her completely without any show of skin, she still managed to look desirable. Rohit's wife took Ravi's breath away, and he felt the blood rush to his face at the mere sight of her. And Ravi desired Nita that very instant.

"Dinner is served," the butler announced, shortly after Ravi's guests had arrived.

They proceeded to the dining room where Ravi's daughter joined them at the dinner table.

"This is my daughter, Minal."

Ravi introduced his daughter to his guests.

Minal was a charming young lady who turned out to be quite a head turner. She was a stunning beauty who was bound to have men falling for her like nine pins.

"I am pleased to meet you." Rohit acknowledged Minal. "And what are you currently doing?" He asked her.

"I'm currently doing my Masters in Business Administration from the Indian School of Business, Hyderabad," Minal replied.

"And what are your plans once you've received your MBA degree?"

Rohit asked Ravi's daughter.

"Well, I'll probably join a reputed Corporate House," Minal said. "I don't believe in wasting my MBA degree by remaining unemployed."

"And it's good to hear that you want to work after graduation as women are equally on par with their male counterpart in today's world. And they are no longer content with merely keeping home and managing the kitchen," Rohit averred.

"Being a homemaker is not my cup of tea, and I would soon be bored to death," Minal stated.

"And I second that," Ravi butted in, as he regarded his daughter fondly. Minal was his favorite child, and he was a tad biased towards her.

#

The meal was a complete Indian fare, with the main course comprising of rice and dal along with mutton curry and fish fry topped with sweetened yogurt. They were served delicious home-made carrot halwa for dessert. And the diners could not resist taking a second helping of the scrumptious sweet.

Nita could barely sit through the meal as she was acutely aware of Ravi's piercing eyes, and she was uncomfortable under his intense scrutiny. Ravi appeared to be paying more attention to her rather than to the meal, and he seemed to be more interested in gazing at her instead of enjoying the fare.

They moved back to the lounge after dinner. And once they had settled down on the couch, they were served Liqueur in delicate China cups.

Ravi brought out a Havana Cigar from the case, and he dangled it loosely from his lips. And although he had no intention of smoking the cigar, it was but a mere distraction to keep his desires in check. Nita had a heady effect on him, and he feared that he would soon spin out of control.

#

It was well past midnight when Rohit and his wife took leave of their host.

"Drive safe," Ravi said to his guests before they departed from the apartment.

"Yes, we will," Rohit affirmed.

They bid their host goodnight before stepping into the elevator and exiting the building. And they headed towards their car which was parked alongside the kerb.

Nita boarded the vehicle and sat on the passenger seat, while Rohit took the wheel. He soon started the engine and shifted gear before revving up and driving away.

Ravi stood mesmerized by the window sans averting his gaze from the couple as he watched the duo all along. And he was rooted to the spot until the silver Mercedes drove away, and the vehicle disappeared completely out of sight.

CHAPTER 13

"I know all about Rahul and you. In fact, I've known about it all along."

Ravi said to Rohit whilst they were having coffee at the bistro.

"Excuse me," Rohit retorted.

"I know about your relationship with Rahul," Ravi reiterated.

"What do you mean?" Rohit asked Ravi. "And what are you talking about?" He queried.

"Oh, come now. Stop pretending you don't know what I mean. And let's not play games here. You know very well what I'm referring to," Ravi averred.

"No, I really have no idea what you are implying," Rohit said. "You appear to be talking in riddles."

"You see, Rahul confided in me and he told me just about everything. And that includes about the two of you as well. Rahul and I go back a long way and there were no secrets between us. I knew that Rahul was bi-sexual, and I must mention here that you are not the first man who he slept with," Ravi stated.

"It was Rahul who pressurized me into the relationship, and I had no choice but to give in," Rohit replied.

Rohit and Rahul had shared a physical relationship, and they were bedfellows. And they met regularly after work to indulge their carnal craving. Rahul was instrumental for the carnal alliance which he initiated under the threat of jeopardizing Rohit's job. And Rohit had no option but to oblige. No one, however, had any inkling of their carnal liaison. And their respective spouses were completely in the dark about their physical intimacy.

"There's always a choice. After all, Rahul didn't exactly put a gun to your head and force you to yield to his demand," Ravi stated.

"Well maybe not, but then he threatened to put my job on the line. And that's just as bad if not worse," Rohit said.

"Well, that's your interpretation. But how do you feel about having blood on your hands?" Ravi asked.

"What do you mean?" Rohit queried.

"Both Rahul and Gita are dead on account of you, and you are responsible for their deaths," Ravi said.

"How so?" Rohit asked.

"Gita got to know about Rahul's relationship with you, and she threatened to leave him. And that would have been detrimental to his career since Gita's father is a very influential person with connections in all the right places. They had a huge row on the night they died, and it ended with Rahul shooting Gita dead before he turned the gun upon himself. I lied earlier when I said that Gita had shot Rahul. In fact, it was the other way around. And I fabricated the housekeeper since Sapna was off duty that night, and she was away when the incident occurred.

"When Rahul called to tell me of what he had done, I tried to calm him down, but he was too distraught to listen to anyone. And even before I could end the conversation, I heard a gunshot in the background, and I knew that it was all over. Rahul had turned the gun upon himself and he had blown his brains out, and he died instantly. It was your relationship with Rahul that killed both him and his wife." Ravi elucidated, and he endeavored to enlighten Rohit about the exact circumstances which had led to the twin deaths.

"It's not mine but Rahul's fault that they are both dead since it was he who was responsible for our relationship," Rohit said. "And he is equally to blame for their deaths."

"Well, whatever it may be that doesn't change the fact that it was your relationship with Rahul that killed him and his wife. And, therefore, you are indirectly responsible for their deaths," Ravi affirmed.

"Even so, I never meant for things to end the way it did," Rohit declared.

"That's fine by me, but what do you suppose will happen once others learn of the truth?"

Ravi asked Rohit.

"No one need ever know the truth. And besides it's all over now," Rohit replied.

"Are you quite certain that no one will ever learn the reason behind Rahul's death? And that nobody will find out what led him to commit suicide before murdering his wife?" Ravi asked. "The truth is hard to hide as it has a way of getting out somehow."

"The truth need never be known should the two of us choose to keep our mouths shut, and we decide to remain mum," Rohit answered.

"Well then, how about we make a deal? I promise not to tell anyone why Rahul killed himself and his wife, provided you return the favor I've done you," Ravi declared.

"Alright, I think that's fair enough and we have ourselves a deal. However, there's one thing that I do need to know though. Were you the one who sent me the photographs? And are you the anonymous sender of the racy snapshots?"

Rohit asked Ravi.

"What photographs are you talking about?"

Ravi queried in turn. And he looked pretty surprised.

"I'm talking about the photographs of Rahul and me together. And it was pure voyeurism on our part that drove us to click those pictures. Someone managed to lay their hands on those private pictures, and they tried to blackmail me with them," Rohit said.

"As a matter of fact, it was I who sent those pictures to you," Ravi stated.

"And how did you get the photos in the first place since I saw Rahul destroy them in my presence. And how did the pictures manage to surface even after they were destroyed?"

Rohit asked Ravi.

"Rahul made copies of the photos before destroying them, and he gave them to me for safekeeping. I suspect he intended to blackmail you with the pictures in the event of you ending the relationship before he did," Ravi answered.

"That explains the appearance of the photos even after they were destroyed," Rohit remarked. "By the way, did you take the pictures from the office safe?" He asked Ravi. "They somehow managed to disappear from where they were kept."

"No, and why would I take back the photographs I blackmailed you with?" Ravi queried.

"I don't know. But since you are the only one apart from me who has access to my safe, I assumed that you had taken the photos," Rohit replied.

"Well then, it's not me," Ravi affirmed. "And that means you've someone else to worry about besides me," he added.

"Yes, I suppose you're right. By the way, was it you who sent me the innuendo filled e-mail and the anonymous letter as well?"

"Yes, it was I who sent you both the e-mail as well as the letter," Ravi said.

"Well, I must say you surprise me as I didn't quite expect you to resort to something of the sort. And I'm sorry to have to tell you this, but you certainly disappoint me." Rohit expressed his disapproval of the modus operandi adopted by Ravi, and he let the latter know that he was disgusted with him for resorting to blackmail.

"Then get over it. Anyways, let's now discuss your part of the bargain."

"And what do you want from me?"

Rohit asked Ravi.

"I'm sure you already know," Ravi answered.

"No, I am afraid, I don't."

"Nita," Ravi said.

"What about Nita?" Rohit asked.

"I'm sure you know that I am interested in your wife," Ravi reiterated.

"As a matter of fact, I wasn't even aware that you were interested in Nita until you just mentioned it to me," Rohit replied.

"I'd like to have your wife at my pleasure and no questions asked. And you know what I mean by that," Ravi said.

"I am afraid that won't be possible since Nita would never agree to anything of the sort. She is too much of a prude to indulge in any sort of a physical relationship outside of marriage. And I suspect it's her small town upbringing that's responsible for her narrow mindset," Rohit stated.

"Then that's your problem and not mine since it's up to you to convince your wife. And I've been planning for this ever since I met Nita," Ravi stated.

"What do you mean?" Rohit asked.

"It was I who instigated Rahul to enter into a relationship with you so that I would have some kind of leverage over you. And I was also instrumental for your out of turn elevation when Pramod resigned, and it was I who was behind your promotion subsequent to Rahul's death. In fact, you owe both your promotions to me. All this was done with an eye on your wife since I used you as bait to get to Nita," Ravi said.

"I'll be damned. I had no idea that you were such a scheming fox," Rohit exclaimed.

"Well, that's just the way I am. When I set my heart on something, I make sure that I go all out to get what I want. And I give a damn whether it's by fair means or foul. Or whether it's right or wrong," Ravi averred. "All I'm concerned about is the end result."

"And, I can see that now. You clearly have no scruples," Rohit said.

"You can analyze my character for all I care as it doesn't bother me. I am only interested in your wife, and I don't give a shit just how I go about getting her. The ball is now in your court and it's up to you to make a decision. You can either choose to indulge me and hold on to your position, or be ready to go job hunting," Ravi retorted.

#

"Are you even listening to yourself? And do you even realize what you are saying? Do you have any idea what you are asking me to do?" Nita asked Rohit when she was told that she would be required to indulge his boss. She was appalled to know that she would have to be at Ravi's pleasure from now on, and that she would be required to gratify Ravi and to satiate his carnal needs from henceforth. She was pretty certain that Rohit had lost his mind as no husband in his right senses would proposition his wife for his boss.

"Yes, I am fully aware of what I'm asking of you. All I'm telling you is to learn to please Ravi in whatever manner it takes," Rohit replied.

"Where is this coming from? And when did you turn out to be this monster who has absolutely no qualms about using his wife for his professional gain?"

Nita asked Rohit.

"I'm afraid that's who I have always been. The very reason I married you was for your looks as I was well aware of Ravi's weakness for a pretty face. And I intended to use you to that end when the time eventually came," Rohit replied.

"You are really disgusting," Nita exclaimed. "If papa only knew the kind of man you are, he would never have gotten me married to you."

"Well, your father is dead, and he wouldn't be able to help you in any way, even if he wanted to," Rohit said.

"Anyways, it's against my principles to sell myself to any man," Nita stated.

"To hell with your principles as this is my job that we are talking about. Anyways what's wrong with what I'm asking of you?" He queried.

"Well, just about everything," Nita replied.

"Don't make it sound like it's such a big deal. And it's not that uncommon either since it happens all the time. People use their wives to get ahead in life, and I expect you to do the same for me," Rohit stated.

"I don't give a damn about other men's wives, but I'm certainly not amenable for that sort of an arrangement," she answered.

"And what do you mean?" Rohit demanded.

"I mean that I will not be used by you for your professional gain. And I won't sleep with your boss to enable you to rise in hierarchy," Nita declared.

"Don't you know that I only have both our best interests at heart here? And don't tell me that you don't enjoy the perks which come with my job."

Rohit asked Nita.

"That's not the point here. I will not sell myself so that you can fulfill your ambitions," Nita reiterated.

"You don't get to decide what to do. I'm your husband and you've to listen to me. And you will do as you're told. Anyways, stop acting so demure since you were certainly not a virgin when you married me."

"And what are you trying to say?" Nita demanded.

"I know that the child you miscarried was not mine. You see, I'm sterile as I had contracted mumps as a young man and was told that I could never become a father. That means some other man had to have fathered the child."

"What does that have to do with the present situation anyways? And how is it relevant to the current discussion?" Nita asked.

"I mean to say that you are no great paragon of virtue, and that you certainly don't fool me by putting on that holier than thou act," Rohit averred.

"As you would never understand the circumstances at the time; it would be futile trying to explain anything to you," Nita answered.

"And neither do I wish to know what pushed you into the situation you found yourself in. If you are what it takes for me to keep my job, I'm prepared to make that sacrifice in the interest of both our futures."

Rohit was ruthlessly ambitious and he was ready to go to any extent to fulfill his ambitions. And he was willing to stoop to any length in the pursuit of his goals. He had no scruples about using his wife to ascend the corporate ladder, and he had no qualms about utilizing Nita to reach the pinnacle of success.

CHAPTER 14

Ravi kept glancing at the clock every once in a while, and he could not help checking the time repeatedly to ascertain that the watch was working. The antique grandfather clock appeared to be running unusually slow as the time was ticking at a snail's pace. And the seconds seemed to be crawling by. Ravi was getting more and more impatient by the minute, and he was on razor's edge as he waited for the clock to strike 9 o'clock. He eagerly looked forward to the evening, and even as he awaited the arrival of the said hour with much anticipation; he was fraught with trepidation. And he was as nervous as a gawky teenager who was about to set out on his first date.

He strode to the bar and he poured himself a stiff whisky in a bid to quell his nervousness. And he had barely finished the drink and put down the glass, when he heard the sound of the doorbell ring.

As the butler was away to attend to a sick relative, he was not present to answer the bell.

Ravi proceeded to answer the door. And as he passed the hallway, he paused briefly before the large ornate mirror to have a look at himself. He was proud of the image that he saw reflected in the looking glass, and he could not help admiring his good looks. Ravi was a handsome man who was once a Calvin Kline model, and age had not ravaged his looks. Time had been kind to Ravi and he had managed to retain his good looks despite the passing years, with the receding hairline being the only telltale sign of aging.

The clock struck nine just as Ravi opened the door, and he was amazed by the perfect keeping of time. Rohit had promised Ravi that his wife would be at his apartment by 9 o'clock, and Nita had arrived bang on the dot of nine.

Nita looked an absolute vision, and Ravi felt the blood rush to his face at the mere sight of her. He could not quite recall when a woman had such a mesmerizing effect on him. And had the situation been different, he would have found himself falling head over heels in love with Nita, as women like her were meant to be idolized.

Ravi was bowled over by Nita at the first instance itself, and he could not quite get her out of his head. And ever since he had met Rohit's wife, he was consumed with the thought of her, and he could not stop thinking about her. Even the fact that she was another man's wife did not deter him from obsessing about her or lusting for her. And he had gone through great lengths in order to gain access to Nita by first befriending her husband and earning his confidence, before stooping to the abysmal level of blackmail.

He had not spared his friendship either in his obsessive pursuit of Rohit's wife as it was he who had blown the lid off Rahul's relationship with Rohit. And he had betrayed his long time friend by revealing everything to the latter's wife. He had paid Gita a courtesy call at her home whilst her husband was away on a business trip. And during the course of their conversation he mentioned about Rahul's carnal alliance with Rohit. Gita, however, accused him of lying and she refused to believe him initially, but once she was shown the raunchy pictures as proof, she was quite convinced that he was telling her the truth. Ravi's spilling of the beans had led to the fatal row between husband and wife, and it was all because of him that they were both dead. And though the death of his dear friend and wife weighed heavily upon Ravi's conscience, it was but a small price to pay for the vision that now stood before him.

Ravi could not wait to get into bed with Nita and to feel the touch of her naked body against his. He wanted to teach her a thing or two between the sheets. Ravi longed to get his hands on Nita … to gently undress her….to drink in every detail of her naked body, before finally taking her. And he felt a faint stirring in his loins as the warm desire coursed through him.

#

Nita was like a frightened deer that stood before the hunter as she waited for Ravi to strike for the kill. Her heart pounded thunderously as she cowered before him since she could not bear the thought of him touching her. She prayed that the ground would open up and swallow her, and that she would miraculously vanish before Ravi could lay his hands upon her.

She had tried to reason with Rohit against coercing her into a carnal liaison with Ravi but to no avail, as her husband would not hear of it. She was told that the very purpose of wedding her was to capitalize on her beauty, and to take advantage of her good looks. And Rohit intended to use Nita to that end in the pursuit of his goals.

Nita had mulled leaving Rohit and she considered ending the marriage but she was, however, not at liberty to make that choice. Her father's will clearly stipulated that the inheritance would be hers subject to her remaining married, and should she choose to leave Rohit, the entire estate, including the manor, would pass on to a trust that was set up in her mother's name. Nita stood to lose everything in the event of her walking out on her husband as she would forfeit her right to her father's estate. And not only would she be left penniless, she would be rendered homeless as well. The only option before her was to resort to the begging bowl, and that was certainly not an enviable proposition.

She had toyed with the idea of snuffing out Rohit's life. And she even made an attempt to smother him with a pillow while he was asleep before abandoning her morbid mission. Better sense had prevailed upon her in the nick of time, and she realized that she was being foolish in her desperation to rid herself of her husband since she would never get away with murder. And she reckoned that she was looking at the possibility of being incarcerated for homicide; doomed to spend the remainder of her days in captivity behind prison walls. As she was pushed to a corner with no means of escape; Nita decided to resign herself to her fate.

#

Ravi did not waste any time trying to make small talk with Rohit's wife nor did he attempt to exchange any pleasantries with her. Nita was here for one purpose only, and he hoped to make the most of it before the night was through. He resolved not to allow her to leave until he had his fill and was sated. Ravi was very gentle with Nita, and he proceeded slowly. He began with her face before gradually traversing along her naked body until he found what he desired.

Nita, however, lay impassive and dead, and she remained indifferent to what was being done to her.

CHAPTER 15

Ravi arrived at the gymnasium for his work out, and as he had reached the fitness center much earlier than was usual, the place was rather empty at this time of the morning. And there was hardly anyone present at the gymnasium at this hour of the day. He saw a middle aged couple briskly cycling on the stationary exercise bike, while a mother and her twin teenage daughters were working the dumb bells, apart from a young man who was running on the treadmill. None of the exercisers were familiar faces as this was not the regular crowd he usually met when he arrived for his daily exercise routine.

He looked out for his personal trainer, but Jimmy was yet to arrive for the day. And since he did not want to wait until his personal trainer showed up, Ravi commenced his exercise sans Jimmy. He boarded the treadmill next to the young man and he started to work out at a steady pace, before gradually increasing the speed on the exercise equipment and trying his best to keep pace with it. Ravi stepped up the pace of his running to synchronize with the high speed of the treadmill, and even as he tried to keep up with the machine, he felt rather out of breath and tired. However, despite the tad of exhaustion and the slight breathlessness, he made no attempt to slow down nor did he stop running, but he continued to work out at the same frenzied pace until he suddenly collapsed. Ravi fell off the treadmill on to the floor, and he soon lost consciousness.

Seeing Ravi lying unconscious on the floor, the young man who was working out next to him stepped off the treadmill at once. And he rushed to Ravi's assistance. He tried his best to revive the former, but without much success. Realizing that the situation was rather serious, he decided to take Ravi to the hospital. He dialed the ambulance service. "I'm calling from Pluto Fitness Center located at Nepean Sea Road. There has been an accident. Could you please send a vehicle immediately to this address in order to get the victim to the hospital?" He said.

The ambulance arrived shortly after the call was made.

Ravi was still unconscious when the paramedics lifted him off the floor and placed him on the stretcher. He was taken to Jaslok Hospital on Peddar Road where he was examined by the doctor. And when he regained consciousness, he found that he was lying on a hospital bed, but he was not alone. The young man from the gymnasium had accompanied him to the hospital, and he had remained by his side until he had come to.

"Thank goodness you are alright. You gave us a terrible fright when you passed out while running on the treadmill, and lost consciousness," the young man said.

"That's really awful. Any idea what happened to me?" Ravi asked.

"Well, according to the doctors, your blood pressure appeared to have suddenly plummeted as a result of which you fainted. But the good news is that you will be alright so there's no need for you to worry," the Good Samaritan stated.

"That's terrible indeed since something of this sort has never happened to me before. And I am a bit embarrassed as well at the panic I caused by passing out at the gym." Ravi said. "Did you arrange for me to be brought to the hospital?"

"Yes, I did."

The stranger affirmed.

"And I'm grateful to you for that. Thank you for all your help." Ravi expressed his gratitude to the stranger for the aid that the latter had rendered to him.

"Well, think nothing of it. It's the least that I could do when I saw you lying unconscious," the stranger answered.

"By the way, I'm Ravi." He introduced himself to the young man.

"And I'm Amar, pleased to make your acquaintance." Amar acknowledged Ravi's introduction." By the way, is there someone who I could call?"

"Yes, as a matter of fact; there is. I'd like you to get in touch with my brother, Ashwin." Ravi gave Amar his brother's telephone number. "And, would you be kind enough to remain with me until he arrives?"

"Yes, of course. I won't leave until your brother arrives," Amar affirmed, before proceeding to make the phone call.

Amar placed the call to Ashwin from his cell phone. "I'm calling on behalf of your brother, Ravi. He has been admitted to Jaslok Hospital." He proceeded to apprise Ashwin of Ravi's condition.

Ashwin arrived at the hospital shortly. "I came as quickly as I could. And I cannot thank you enough for the help that you extended to my brother." He expressed his gratitude to Amar for his assistance.

"I was just doing my duty as a fellow human," Amar answered.

"And it's very kind of you to remain with my brother until I showed up," Ashwin reiterated.

"It's the least that I could do," Amar said.

"I'll take over from here now and you can leave, but we certainly owe you one. Should you require our help at any time, please feel free to call." Ashwin handed Amar his business card.

Ravi did not meet Amar at the gymnasium after that morning; neither did he hear from him after that day. He looked out for Amar every time he went for his work out, but he never saw the latter again after that morning. Amar had appeared like a guardian angel on that fateful morning, and he had taken good care of Ravi. Ravi was greatly indebted to Amar, and he wanted to repay the debt that he owed to the Good Samaritan.

#

Ravi heard from Amar a couple of months later when he called him at the office.

"I took the liberty of taking your number from your brother as I wanted to get in touch with you. And I hope you don't mind me calling you at your place of work," Amar stated.

"No, not at all," Ravi affirmed.

"I'd like to see you sometime when you are free," Amar said.

"Well, you could drop by the office tomorrow," Ravi replied.

"Are you sure that's alright?" Amar asked Ravi "I don't want to disturb you while you are at work."

"Yes, of course. It's no problem at all," Ravi averred.

"What time should I be there?"

Amar asked Ravi.

"Around mid-morning should be fine," Ravi stated.

Amar arrived at Ravi's office around 11.00 A.M. the following morning.

"I'm sorry to take up your time since I know that you are a very busy person," Amar stated. "And it's awfully kind of you to agree to see me." He apologized to Ravi for imposing upon his time.

"No, that's quite alright. Besides, I can always spare the time for you," Ravi said. "By the way, I look out for you every time I go to the gym, but I haven't seen you since that morning."

"I've cancelled my membership at the gym, and that's the reason why we've not run into each other again," Amar replied.

"I was pleasantly surprised to hear from you as it's been quite a while since we met. Is this just a courtesy visit?"

Ravi asked Amar.

"No, as a matter of fact, I've come to ask you for a favor," Amar said. "That's if it's alright with you," he added, as an afterthought.

"Well then, what can I do for you?" Ravi queried.

"I hope you don't think I'm taking undue advantage of you, but I was wondering whether you had a job opening for me in your organization." Amar requested for a job. "And I've brought my resume with me just in case you would like to have a look at my CV."

"Where are you presently employed?"

Ravi asked Amar about his current employment.

"At present I am unemployed, and I'm helping my grandfather run his business," Amar replied.

"And do you have any previous work experience?" Ravi asked.

"I worked for a reputed MNC in Bangalore, but then I had to quit my job when I moved to Mumbai as they don't have a branch in the city," Amar said.

"Hand me your CV and I'll see what I can do. However, I can't commit to anything without checking the job scenario first. I will pass on your resume to HRD and ask them to get in touch with you should there be a suitable vacancy. But I don't make any promises, and I don't want you to get your hopes up too high lest you should end up being disappointed." Ravi was non committal whilst considering Amar's request for a job in the organization since he did not want to give the latter any false assurances. And although he was keen to help Amar find employment, he was wary of making a promise that he was uncertain of fulfilling.

"Of course, I understand. And I won't take offence if nothing comes up. I'm only taking a chance here," Amar replied. "And thank you for sparing the time for me." He soon took leave of Ravi.

#

Amar received a call a week later in response to his job application when he was asked to appear for an interview. "I am calling from Stan Express Bank. The Executive Vice-President would like to see you regarding a job opening. Could you meet him tomorrow around 4.00 P.M.? And bring your testimonials along with you." He was told.

Amar arrived at Stan Express Bank a little before 4.00 P.M. He was told at the reception to proceed to the EVP's office where he was ushered into the latter's room by Raveena.

"I've gone through your CV, and I must say that I am pretty impressed. And you are exactly the person I'm looking for. This is for the post of an Assistant. And should all go well, you will be working for me," Rohit stated, before he proceeded to conduct a thorough interview of the candidate. "Congratulations, you've passed the test with flying colours, and I'd like you to join at the earliest." He offered Amar the position of Assistant upon successful completion of the interview.

"Well, I would be able to join from Monday." Amar stated his willingness to join the organization after the weekend.

"That's great," Rohit averred."I look forward to you being a member of my team."

Amar started work at Stan Express Bank on Monday morning, and he was allotted a cubicle next to Raveena. Amar and Raveena, however, did not seem to hit it off too well as they took an instant dislike to each other.

Amar soon proved to be an invaluable asset, and Rohit began to rely completely on him.

Rohit was glad that he had hired Amar since the latter appeared to be tailor-made for the job. And he could not have asked for anyone better to fill the position. "You seem to have learned the ropes rather quickly, and I must say that I'm pretty impressed with you." He complimented Amar on the latter's learning skills.

"Well, that seems to be my forte. I once worked as the overseer of a coffee plantation in Mercara, and despite being an absolute greenhorn, I managed to do justice to the job," Amar replied.

"Are you serious?" Rohit asked

"Yes," Amar reiterated.

"You really do surprise me. I had absolutely no idea that you worked on an estate in Mercara." Rohit stated. "In fact, I had no inkling that you were ever in Coorg. Tourists visit the place to enjoy the scenic beauty, but not to take up a job there."

"Well, that was a long time ago. And it was a very short stint," Amar said.

"And why did you quit the job?"

Rohit asked Amar.

"It wasn't my cup of tea since I wasn't cut out to rough it out on an estate. I took up the job as a challenge before I realized that it was a big mistake, and I soon wanted to quit," Amar answered.

"Same goes for me too since I opted for a corporate job instead of managing my father's estate," Rohit stated.

"And was your father happy with your decision?"

"Goodness no, rather it invoked his ire as he hoped that I would take over the reins of the estate from him someday, and that he would finally be able to lead a laid-back life. However, when he realized that I would be miserable managing the plantation, he decided to let me have my way."

"I see. I suppose all's well that ends well."

"Yes, you're right. By the way, my wife happens to be from Mercara and I'm sure she would be happy to meet you as you were once a resident of her hometown. Why don't you come home one of these days and the two of you can reminisce about the place?" Rohit said.

"I'd feel awkward dropping in at my superior's residence for a social evening." Amar politely declined Rohit's invitation.

"Nonsense, I'm not your boss outside of the office, but only your colleague," Rohit stated.

"I will try to bear that in mind," Amar said.

"Good. In fact, why don't you come home for dinner tomorrow? We could leave together after work."

"Are you sure?" Amar asked.

"Yes, of course, and drop the formality."

#

"By the way, I'm bringing a guest home for dinner tomorrow night," Rohit said to Nita. "And I hope it's alright with you since I didn't give you any prior notice? Will you be terribly inconvenienced by this last minute decision?" He asked his wife.

"That's alright. And who is coming over for dinner tomorrow?"

Nita asked Rohit.

"It's no one you know. I've invited one of my colleagues from the office," Rohit replied.

"And what do you want cooked for dinner? Is there anything in particular that you would like to have served?"

Nita asked Rohit.

"It would be better to keep the meal simple, and don't make it too elaborate. I feel a traditional Coorg spread should be fine. The main course could comprise of rice balls and pork curry, while you could serve caramel custard for dessert," Rohit stated.

"Are you sure that would be fine? I mean there is hardly any variety."

"Yes, that's precisely what our guest wants served since that's his favorite Coorg dish," Rohit averred.

"Alright," Nita affirmed.

#

Nita was caught completely unawares when she saw the person her husband had invited to dine with them. And her heart stopped short of beating when she met their dinner guest. Amar was the last person whom Nita had expected to show up at her home. And it was like seeing a ghost from the past; a ghost that had never been completely exorcised.

Amar could not quite believe his eyes when he saw Nita, and he wondered whether he was dreaming. He had no idea that Rohit was married to Nita, and that she was his wife. He had never expected to meet her when he accepted

Rohit's invitation to dine at their home, and he never thought that he would ever see her again. Not only did Nita look as lovely as he had always remembered her to be; she appeared to have grown more beautiful with time. Amar's heart did a somersault and his pulse beat rapidly at the mere sight of Nita, and he could scarcely contain his desire for her. Even after all these years his love for her remained unchanged. And in that instant Amar knew that he had never stopped loving Nita, and that he loved her to this day.

"Nita, meet Amar. And he is my Assistant at the office. Amar, this is my wife, Nita."

Rohit introduced Amar and Nita to each other. He was unaware that the two had history, and that Amar was the father of the child his wife had miscarried.

"Very pleased to meet you, and how are you?"

Amar acknowledged the introduction.

"Very well, thank you."

Nita replied politely.

There were a million questions that each wanted to pose to the other as they were both looking for answers. However, since now was not the time or the occasion to raise those queries, they behaved like complete strangers.

CHAPTER 16

Nita could not resist sneaking a peek at her husband's cell phone while he was in the shower. She was trying to locate Amar's telephone number, and she was pretty certain that Rohit had the number stored in his phone. As her husband had a terrible memory when it came to remembering telephone numbers, all his contacts were listed on the cell phone from where they could be easily accessed when the need arose. Nita scrolled through the exhaustive list of contacts until she found what she was looking for. And once she had made a note of Amar's telephone number, she kept the phone back in its original position so as to avoid arousing her husband's suspicions. Since Rohit's official mobile phone contained only his business contacts, Nita's curiosity would be suspect.

As Nita could not risk telephoning Amar from either her cell phone or the residential landline for fear of the call being traced back to her, she placed the call from a public booth. And she telephoned Amar from a pay phone that was located across the street.

Amar was about to sit down to lunch when Nita called, and as the number flashing on the telephone screen did not appear to be familiar, he rejected the call. And since he did not wish to be disturbed during the meal, he declined to take the call. However, when the caller dialed him repeatedly in spite of being rejected each time, he decided to answer his phone. And he could not quite believe his ears when he heard the voice at the other end.

"Nita is that really you?" He asked.

"Yes, it's me here," Nita replied.

"How have you been? It's been such a long time, and we couldn't really talk the other night," Amar said.

"Yes I know, and that's the reason why I'd like to see you again," Nita stated.

"Well, I'd like to meet you too. But then do you think it's a good idea considering the history between us?"

Amar asked Nita.

"Well, we could meet as friends. And there is no harm in two friends meeting. Is there?" Nita asked.

"No, I suppose not," Amar replied.

"And besides I'd like to clear the air between us considering the way you disappeared from my life."

"Well, alright then, let's meet one of these days," Amar said." But what would your husband say should he discover about our tryst? Would he not object to our meeting?" He asked.

"Rohit doesn't have to know about our rendezvous since this is my personal business, and it's got nothing to do with him," Nita answered.

"Are you sure that it is alright as it would be rather awkward for me at work otherwise?" Amar asked. "After all, your husband is my superior."

"Yes, absolutely; this is none of my husband's business," Nita reiterated.

"And where would you like to meet me? How about we meet up at the coffee shop once I'm done at work?" Amar asked Nita." I'll wait at Café Coffee Day. I think that would be ideal."

"I don't think Café Coffee Day is a good idea. The coffee shop is too public a place and anyone could be there. And I don't want us to be seen together for fear of our meet being misconstrued and leading to unpleasant gossip. Honestly, I'd be more comfortable meeting you somewhere more private where no one can see us," Nita answered.

"Well, in that case, the best place would be my apartment," Amar averred.

"Very well, then I shall meet you at your place."

"And when would you like to come over?"

Amar asked Nita.

"The next weekend should be fine since Rohit will be away on a business trip," she replied.

"In that case, would Sunday be alright?" He asked.

"Yes, absolutely," Nita affirmed.

"I'll message you the address. And I shall look forward to seeing you on Sunday."

#

Nita hired a cab to take her to Ridgeway Towers, and she rode a taxi to reach Amar's apartment. "I need to get to Nepean Sea Road, and could you take a longer route. And don't worry about the meter since I'm ready to pay the fare without haggling." She said to the taxi driver whilst instructing him to take a circuitous route.

"Very well," the taxi driver affirmed, before acceding to Nita's request and choosing a longer route to reach her destination. He first drove to Marine Drive and then along Chowpatty before turning towards Walkeshwar to proceed to Nepean Sea Road. And when the taxi drew to a halt at the kerb outside Ridgeway Towers, Nita handed the driver a handsome tip over the meter before alighting from the vehicle. "Keep the change," she stated.

Nita stepped out of the taxi and entered the building before proceeding towards the elevator. She rode the express elevator to the sixth floor to reach Amar's apartment. And she was a tad nervous when she rang the door bell as there were a million butterflies fluttering in her stomach.

The bell was answered shortly by Amar who greeted Nita at the door. "I'm glad that you could make it," he said. "I was rather apprehensive about your visit, and was afraid that you would cancel at the last moment."

"I've been looking forward to this day, and wouldn't have missed it for anything in the world," Nita replied.

Amar invited Nita inside before introducing her to his grandfather.

"Dadaji, this is Nita. Remember I told you about her?"

"You are even more beautiful than my grandson described you to be. In fact, Amar's description doesn't do enough justice to your looks. I didn't realize that you were so lovely." Jagdeep complimented Nita on her beauty. He found her to be quite stunning, and he could not quite take his eyes off her. He realized that Nita was a raving beauty, and he could now understand why his grandson was still madly in love with her.

Nita blushed at Jagdeep's compliment, and she took an instant liking to Amar's grandfather. "How are you feeling now? I understand that you've been a bit under the weather lately?" She enquired about Jagdeep's health.

"I had a mild bout of influenza and managed to recover well from the flu. Anyways I'm old now and I suppose ill health comes with the territory," Jagdeep quipped.

"You should take good care of your health irrespective of your age," Nita stated sagely.

Jagdeep was aware that his presence made the duo uncomfortable, and he realized that they would be ill at ease while he remained with them. And he wished to give the duo some privacy. "Well, it's time for my evening stroll. And I'm off to the Priyadarshini Park to meet my friends." He expressed his intent to step out of the apartment.

"Are you sure you want to go to the park? And do you really feel up to it considering that you've been in bed all morning?"

Amar asked Jagdeep.

"Yes, I feel absolutely fine and a breath of fresh air will do me some good," Jagdeep replied.

"Are you certain that you feel alright to go for a stroll outside? Or are you just getting away to give us some privacy?" Amar queried.

"Yes, I'm pretty certain that I feel fit to go for a walk in the park," Jagdeep reiterated. "And I'm looking forward to meeting my friends."

"Call me if you need me to come and fetch you," Amar said.

"Don't worry about me. And besides it's just across the street. The two of you are meeting after a long time, and I'm sure you have a lot of catching up to do. So, make the most of it while I'm gone," Jagdeep stated. He soon left the apartment to proceed to the park.

Amar led Nita to the couch before sitting down beside her. He longed to take her in his arms and kiss her passionately on the lips but he let that thought pass. They were no longer the people they once were, and much water had flown under the bridge since. It had been a long time and everything had changed between them. Nita was now a married woman, and she was another man's wife.

"Nita, I want you to know that I did not betray your trust by walking out on you and our unborn child," Amar stated.

"Yes, I know that now since Ganga told me everything after papa passed away," Nita answered. "But, why did you vanish without even wishing me goodbye?" She asked.

"When your father realized that he could not kill me, he ordered me out of his property that very instant. If I so much as lingered even for a moment he was going to have me arrested on charges of rape. And given the impending threat, I had little choice but to leave the place immediately and disappear from your life; even though that was the last thing I wanted to do."

"I never imagined that papa could be so heartless."

Nita remarked when she learned that her father had resorted to unscrupulous measures to banish Amar from her life.

"And I tried to get in touch with you by writing a letter every day and kept waiting for a reply, but when I never heard from you I slipped into depression, and I tried to drown my sorrow in drink. But when alcohol didn't help ease the pain of my heartbreak, I wanted to end my misery by killing myself. And I tried to commit suicide by hanging myself from the ceiling fan, but timely intervention from my mother saved me. When mamma walked in on me trying to kill myself, she lost no time in cutting the rope, and she rushed me to the hospital. Had there been any delay on her part in getting me timely medical aid, I would've died. And I was saved in the nick of time." Amar spoke of his suicide bid when Nita remained incommunicado.

"That's because your letters never reached me. And it was only years later that I learned about them," Nita said.

"And what about the child that you were expecting, did your father force you to have an abortion?"

Amar asked Nita.

"Papa got me married as soon as he could. In fact, I got married within a month of your going away, and came to Mumbai soon after my wedding. I was certain that Rohit would not suspect my pregnancy as I was married and there are instances of women conceiving right away. However, I was wrong to imagine that Rohit could be fooled into believing that he was the father of the child I was expecting since he knew from the start that the baby was not his. As Rohit is sterile, he can never father a child."

"Does that mean that you gave birth to the baby? And what happened to our child once it was born?" Amar queried.

"I suffered a miscarriage shortly after coming to Mumbai, and I lost the baby. And I suppose losing the baby was a blessing in disguise as Rohit would never have forgiven our child for not being his," Nita answered.

"Are you happy and content in your marriage? And is Rohit a good husband?"

Amar asked Nita.

"Yes, I'm very happy. And Rohit is a wonderful husband. In fact, I have a perfect marriage." Nita lied about being happy with Rohit since she did not want Amar to know that she was trapped in a bad marriage. As it would break his heart to learn of her ordeal to satiate Ravi's carnal needs at the behest of her husband; she decided to spare him the truth.

"Well, I'm glad to hear that you are happily married, and that your husband takes good care of you. You know that I'd hate it if it was otherwise," Amar stated.

"I've stayed much longer than I had intended to, and I really think I should leave now before my husband's call comes through. Rohit is away on business, and he comes via the webcam every evening to speak to me, and his suspicions will be aroused if I'm not at home to take his call," Nita stated.

Amar rose to let Nita out of the apartment. But even before he could leave his seat, Nita pulled him towards her, and she kissed him passionately on the lips. Amar's will power crumbled at the touch of Nita's soft lips. He was starved of her for so long that he wilted; and he responded to her kiss. And before they knew it, they were making love on the couch. Nita surrendered completely to Amar as it felt right to have him make love to her.

CHAPTER 17

Nita silently slipped out of the apartment when Rohit was having his afternoon siesta. And she left the residence whilst her husband was still asleep. Rohit would not awaken until late in the evening, and she hoped to be back at home well before he rose from his slumber.

She soon emerged from the building, and headed towards the car that was parked alongside the kerb. A blue Mercedes Benz was waiting for her at the corner of the street. And the chauffeur had specific instructions to pick her up.

"Good morning, Madam."

The chauffeur greeted Nita before opening the rear door of the car to allow his passenger to board the vehicle.

"Good morning Narayan, and how have you been?"

Nita acknowledged the chauffeur's greeting.

"Very well madam. And where are we going today?" Narayan asked. "I was told to take you to the race course."

"That's right. I need to get to the Mahalaxmi Race Course," Nita stated.

"Yes, of course," Narayan affirmed. He soon started the engine and shifted gear before joining the stream of traffic, and driving away. And another vehicle followed closely behind them.

Nita sank back in the cushioned seat of the luxury vehicle, and she had quick forty winks while the car meandered through traffic. And she dozed on the ride to the race course. Nita was unaware that she was being tailed.

They arrived at the Mahalaxmi Race Course shortly. The chauffeur brought the vehicle to a grinding halt and stepped out of the car, before holding the door open for his passenger to alight.

Nita alighted from the Mercedes and she proceeded towards the Gallops Restaurant that was situated on the grounds of the race course. And she entered the restaurant to find Amar having a sandwich. Nita joined Amar at the table.

"I ordered Club Sandwiches and coffee as I was rather hungry, and I made it a double order since you were coming. I hope that's alright with you," Amar said.

"Yes, of course, anything's fine, although I'm not very hungry since I had a rather heavy lunch. I don't want anything to eat, and would prefer to have a cup of coffee," Nita replied.

"Well, suit yourself. By the way, there are races on at the race course today. I was wondering whether you would you be interested in watching the races? Or would you rather go someplace else?"

Amar asked Nita.

"I'm only interested in your company. And it doesn't matter whether it's at the race course or anywhere else," Nita averred.

"Are you sure?" Amar asked. "I know that you are averse to gambling of any kind."

"Well, I'm willing to make an exception for your sake," she replied.

"That's really very generous of you. And I must say I'm touched," he said.

"Well, have you decided which horse you are going to lay your bet on?"

Nita asked Amar.

"I'm going to lay a wager on a horse running the first race as I don't wish to spend the whole afternoon at the race course," Amar replied.

Amar picked up the tab at the restaurant, and he paid the bill before they left the eatery. He then proceeded to the betting enclosure at the race course to place his bet on an equine participating in the first racing event.

"Yes sir?"

The clerk at the booking window enquired when Amar approached him.

"I'd like to place a bet on the first race. And I wish to lay a wager on the horse, Joyous." Amar placed his bet before they entered the racing arena and took their place in the stands.

The horses were brought from the paddocks shortly, and they soon took their position at the gate. There were six horses in the race, and Joyous was allotted Gate Number 6. A bell was rung to announce the start of the race, and with the ringing of the bell, the gates sprung open. The horses instantly set into motion as they commenced the race, and they were being egged on by their respective jockeys to take the lead. Joyous was trailing far behind the other runners as the mare was coming last.

"The horses have now taken off and the race has begun. We have Mayur ridden by Bandish in the lead, while Royalty ridden by Manish is a close second, followed by Porus ridden by Laxman and Darius ridden by Salim whilst Oyster with Pal on the saddle is neck to neck with Joyous ridden by Alan. And they are both coming last."

The commentator announced.

The horses were a mere 600 meters away from the finish line when Joyous suddenly sprang wings. She came out of nowhere and gathered speed as she ran like the wind. Joyous gradually covered the distance between the other horses before overtaking them and gaining in lead. And the mare left the other runners far behind as she galloped ahead to reach the finish line first. Joyous won the race by a handsome length.

"…. the race has been won by Joyous with jockey Alan at the saddle. And the winner is paying odds of 100:1," the commentator concluded.

Amar turned to Nita after the race. "I've won a handsome amount from the wager. You seem to be my lucky charm, and I must bring you to the races more often."

"That's nothing but nonsense as I believe we make our own luck," Nita replied.

Amar collected his winnings before they left the racing arena to proceed to the parking lot. He approached the Blue Mercedes to speak to the chauffeur. "I'll take Nita home, Narayan. And you get back to dadaji since he needs the car." Amar dismissed the chauffeur.

They drove to the National Sports Club of India at Worli.

Amar approached the reception. "I am a member of the club. And I'd like a room for a couple of hours. I know this is very short notice, but I would appreciate it if you could oblige me all the same," he said to the receptionist.

"I will have to first check the availability of a room as we are fully booked," the receptionist replied. She proceeded to check the computer log before obliging Amar. "A room fell vacant this afternoon and it can be allotted to you. However, you will have to vacate the place by late evening since we have a guest arriving early tomorrow morning," she stated, handing Amar the key to the room.

"That's fine," Amar affirmed.

"It's on the third floor. Room No. 303. Do you want to be shown to your room?"

The receptionist asked Amar.

"That's alright. We'll find our way," Amar replied.

Amar escorted Nita to the third floor before they let themselves into the room which was allotted to them.

"Why have you brought me here?"

Nita asked Amar.

"That's because I want some alone time with you. And that's not possible with dadaji always around at home," Amar replied. "Nita, I never stopped loving you. And even though I tried to forget you, no matter how hard I tried, I could never erase you from my memory." He confessed to still being in love with Nita.

"My feelings for you haven't changed, and I never fell out of love with you. But fate, however, willed otherwise, and I ended up being with Rohit," Nita said.

"Why does life have to be so cruel," Amar sighed.

"Let's not go down that road but live in the moment." Nita snuggled against Amar.

Amar enveloped Nita in his arms and he sought her lips before kissing her passionately. He then proceeded to undress her. Amar undid the zipper on Nita's denim skirt, and he unbuttoned her silk blouse before removing the clasp of her lace bra and pulling down her sheer panty. Nita now lay stark naked before him. Amar took in every detail of her body… her alabaster skin, the pear shaped breasts, her cherry red nipples and her glistening down.

"You are still beautiful in every manner." Amar complimented Nita on her sculpted body. And he wanted to make love to her that instant. He proceeded to undress himself. He removed his tee and stepped out of his pants before peeling off his boxers. And he soon joined Nita on the large double bed.

Amar kissed Nita gently on her eyes and he tenderly brushed her pert nose with his lips before crushing her mouth. His tongue then meandered along her naked body until he found her warm depth. Nita gasped with the exquisite pleasure, and she soon reached a climax.

CHAPTER 18

"Nita, I want to feel married to you."

Amar said once they were sated and spent making love.

"And what do you mean?"

Nita asked Amar.

"I know that you are already married but I'd like to go through a ritual in private in spite of that," he said.

"But that doesn't make any sense since nobody would accept the marriage," she averred.

"Yes, I'm aware of that, but I'd like to go through the motions all the same in order to appease my conscience," Amar reiterated.

"And how so?" Nita queried.

"I'd feel less guilty about sleeping with another man's wife," he said.

"And what do you suggest?"

Nita asked Amar.

"We could proceed to the nearest temple where I will apply vermillion on your forehead in the presence of the deity. And I know that it's not much of a ceremony, but that's the least I can do."

"Well, if it makes you happy, I'm open to your suggestion. Although, I don't think it really matters since I already feel that I am one with you," Nita stated.

"Well, it's important to me," Amar reiterated.

"Alright then, let's go and get married before either of us changes our mind," Nita said.

They vacated the room and paid the tariff before checking out of the club. And they proceeded to locate a temple close by.

#

Amar stopped before a temple a short distance away, and he brought the car to a halt outside the House of God. They alighted from the vehicle and entered the place of worship to proceed towards the deity.

The temple was dedicated to the Goddess of Wealth and a beautiful idol of the Goddess Mahalaxmi stood at the shrine. The deity was draped in a gold bordered emerald green silk sari and she was heavily decked with gold ornaments, whilst bright red vermillion adorned her forehead.

"Nita, this is a good omen. Goddess Mahalaxmi herself is going to bear witness to our union," Amar said.

"I only want you to be happy," Nita stated.

"And nothing could make me happier than to be married to you." Amar gathered vermillion from the idol, and he smeared it on Nita's forehead. "I now consider you as my spouse, and we are one from this day onwards. And I want dadaji to bless this union," he said.

"Do you think that's a good idea?"

 Nita asked Amar.

"What do you mean?"

"I am skeptical of dadaji approving of this union."

"And why do you think dadaji would disapprove of this temple wedding?"

Amar asked Nita.

"Well, for starters, I am already married. And this is a sham wedding," Nita said.

"Dadaji loves me unconditionally. And he would never object to anything that I did irrespective of whether it's right or wrong," Amar stated.

"Well, I suppose you are the best judge of dadaji," Nita averred.

"Exactly," Amar affirmed.

They sought the blessings of the deity, and they asked the Goddess to shower them with happiness before departing from the temple.

They emerged from the place of worship and boarded the car to proceed to Ridgeway Towers. And once they had reached the building, Amar parked the car in the garage before leading Nita to the private elevator. They rode the elevator together to the sixth floor, and they stepped into the lobby when the door sprung open.

"I didn't expect you back so soon. And I thought that you'd stay out until much later." Jagdeep said to Amar. "And I'm surprised that you returned home early."

"Well, that was the original plan, but I had a change of heart," Amar said.

"What do you mean?" Jagdeep queried.

"Dadaji, I went through a ritual with Nita."

"And what kind of ritual are you talking about?"

Jagdeep asked his grandson.

"I accompanied Nita to a temple and applied vermillion on her forehead in the presence of the deity. And so technically, she is now my wife," Amar said.

"Are you serious?" Jagdeep queried.

"Yes, dadaji," Amar affirmed.

"And how could you be that stupid. Nita is a married woman and your ritual has no meaning since nobody would recognize this marriage." Jagdeep chided his grandson for his naivety.

"And I'm aware that this union is not legitimate, but I went through it all the same," Amar reiterated. "Dadaji, I don't want you to be judgmental."

"You know that I love you and that I mean well for you. And I don't want to see you get hurt," Jagdeep said.

"Nita and I are meant to be together. And that's why she has come back into my life again." Amar tried to justify his action. "I want you to bless us." He sought his grandfather's good wishes.

Amar and Nita bent down in unison, and they touched Jagdeep's feet.

Jagdeep bestowed his blessings upon the couple, and he wished the duo well. "Now, this calls for a celebration." He brought out a bottle of champagne and raised a toast to his grandson's happiness before presenting Nita with a gift. "Meher wanted to give this to her daughter-in-law, but she never got that opportunity. So now, this is rightfully yours." Jagdeep presented Nita with a diamond necklace.

"It's beautiful but I can't accept such an expensive necklace." Nita declined Jagdeep's gift.

"Nonsense, this is meant for you. And I'd feel very offended should you refuse to accept it," Jagdeep said.

"Alright, but I can't take this necklace home as Rohit would find out, and there would be awkward questions. And since I am a terrible liar, he would soon learn the truth behind it. It would be better for Amar to keep the necklace with him, and I can wear it when I'm here," Nita said.

#

Nita left Amar's apartment shortly, and when she emerged from the building, she had no inkling that she was being spied upon. She was being photographed while exiting Ridgeway Towers and images of her emerging from the building were captured on the camera of a cell phone. Pictures of her leaving the place were uploaded, and they were being sent via email to an interested party.

She hailed a cab to take her home, and her taxi was tailed and followed all the way to her apartment building. And when she alighted from the cab to pay the taxi fare, a phone call was placed to the recipient of the photographs.

Rohit was having his evening cup of tea when Nita arrived at the apartment.

"I didn't find you at home when I woke up from my nap, and I wondered where you had gone," Rohit said, when Nita entered. "And where were you all this while since I had no idea that you were going out?"

"I went to meet a friend, and I'm sorry that I forgot to mention it to you," Nita answered.

"And does this friend have a name?" He asked.

"I went to meet Priya," she replied.

"Are you sure that you went to meet Priya?" Rohit queried.

"Yes, of course," Nita reiterated.

"Stop lying to me that you were with Priya because I know that you were with Amar." Rohit accused his wife of being with his Assistant.

"That's ridiculous, and why on earth would I meet Amar?" Nita asked.

"Because I know that's where you've been. And don't try to deny the truth since I not only have pictures as proof of your presence at Amar's building, but you were also tailed from the time you set out on your rendezvous right up to Ridgeway Towers and back," Rohit stated.

"Did you have me followed?"

Nita asked Rohit.

"Yes, I'm afraid so, I had you trailed all the way right until the time you returned home. In fact, I hired a private detective to keep an eye on you, and he has been following you like a shadow ever since," Rohit replied.

"And why the hell would you have me spied upon anyways?" Nita queried.

"Why else would I have you tailed, but to keep an eye on you?"

"You are despicable to spy on your wife." Nita expressed her disgust at being tailed.

"Well, you didn't leave me with much choice. Since I suspected that you were in a relationship with Amar, I needed concrete evidence to confirm my suspicions before I could confront you with the truth. And these pictures are proof enough that you went to meet him." Rohit showed Nita the pictures of her leaving Amar's building.

"And how did you even find out about us in the first place?" Nita asked.

"I accidentally overheard Amar fix a date with you, and I wasn't sure that I had heard right. And just to make doubly certain that I wasn't mistaken; I checked your cell phone once I got home. And that's when I found the phone calls and the text messages that were exchanged between you and Amar which established my suspicion that the two of you were in a relationship," Rohit elucidated, throwing light on how he had chanced upon Nita's affair with Amar.

"Now that the truth is finally out, I might as well be honest with you. I love Amar and have every intention of leaving you to be with him," Nita declared. "I would have left you when you drove me into Ravi's bed, but the thought of losing my inheritance stopped me from walking out of this marriage. Now that I have Amar, I don't give a damn if I don't get a penny from papa," Nita stated.

"And you must be really naïve if you think that I'd let you go," her husband retorted.

"You've destroyed the very sanctity of this marriage by pushing me into prostitution. So why do you even care should I choose to leave you?" she asked.

"I have my reasons. And besides, you're my golden goose. With you by my side, I can play Ravi like a puppet," Rohit answered.

"That's too bad as my mind is made up and I want out of this marriage. And you can go to hell for all I care," Nita retorted.

"It's interesting to know that you have no qualms about walking out on me. But do you know whether Amar would still be willing to accept you once he learns of your association with Ravi? And would he be willing to forgive you your carnal relationship with Ravi?"

Rohit asked Nita.

"Are you trying to intimidate me by threatening me?" Nita queried.

"I don't issue empty threats unless I have every intention of carrying it out," her husband averred. "And I won't hesitate to tell Amar about Ravi and you."

"Then I will tell Amar that you are instrumental for my association with Ravi, and that it was you who forced me into the relationship. Amar will believe me when I tell him that's the truth."

"Are you quite sure that Amar will believe you when you tell him that you are above blame, because the way I see it you'll come across as a ruthlessly ambitious wife who is willing to do all that it takes to promote her husband's career. And that includes sleeping with his boss."

"Amar knows me well enough to know that it's not true. And he will understand that it was done at your behest," Nita reiterated.

"I'm not so sure that Amar will believe you because people change with time. Amar will probably term you a gold-digger and he'll end up hating you for sleeping with your husband's boss. And is that what you really want? To be hated by the man you love?" Rohit asked.

"No," Nita mumbled.

"Then if you know what's good for you, stay away from Amar. And you won't live to regret it. And this is an ultimatum," Rohit said.

#

Nita ran into Amar a couple of days later at the parking lot of Stan Express Bank building.

"What are you doing here?"

Amar asked Nita.

"I dropped by to see my husband," Nita replied.

"You seem to have become a stranger lately. Is everything alright with you as I haven't seen you or heard from you in a while? And why aren't you returning my phone calls or answering any of my text messages? I miss you," he said.

"I'm sorry if I gave you the wrong impression earlier, but I never meant to rekindle our romance. After all I am a married woman, and I respect the institution of marriage too much to stray," she answered.

"Were you just playing with my feelings all along? And why did you lead me on if you were not serious?"

Amar asked Nita.

"I guess I got carried away seeing you after all these years, and I gave in to my impulses before better sense prevailed upon me and I decided to end the affair," she replied.

"Are you trying to tell me that the time we spent together meant nothing to you at all?" Amar queried.

"I am afraid so," Nita reiterated.

"And what about the ceremony at the temple, did that too not mean anything to you?" He asked.

"I agreed to the ceremony at the temple only to make you happy since it was important to you. And it had no particular significance for me," she replied.

"You really do take me by surprise since it was you who got in touch with me in the first place," Amar said.

"That was for old times' sake," Nita averred.

"And here I was a fool to imagine that nothing had changed between us and that you still loved me. And I was seriously considering setting up home with you. I even sought dadaji's permission to have you move in with us, and despite everything; he agreed for my sake," Amar stated.

"Well, you should have first consulted me before planning for my move into your home," Nita said.

"Yes, I now realize that I should have consulted you before planning for us to be together. And that I was a fool to have taken things for granted." Amar stated sardonically.

"I could never imagine leaving my husband considering the shame it would bring to the family. And papa would probably turn in his grave at the scandal it would cause. I don't want you to ever try to contact me again as you will only hear silence from my end."

Nita wanted to rush into Amar's arms, and she longed to seek refuge in his warm embrace. But since Rohit's threat hung over her like a sword, she was compelled to put up a charade. She asked Amar never to get in touch with her or attempt to see her again. And as she walked away from him, her eyes were swimming with tears.

CHAPTER 19

Jagdeep was at the Law Firm of his solicitors, Amarchand and Associates, to execute his Will. As he was told that his death was imminent and that he was now living on borrowed time, he wanted to put his affairs in order before it was too late. His cancer, which was in remission all this while had relapsed, and he was now terminal and it was only a matter of days before he passed away. And he wished to complete the legalities of his estate before time ran out for him.

Amar had accompanied Jagdeep to the solicitors' office. And he had taken prior permission to stay away from work. Despite Rohit having a rather busy schedule for the day, he was kind enough to give his Assistant time off to attend to personal work.

#

"I want to make sure that no one will be able to contest the Will after I am gone." Jagdeep instructed the senior partner, Amarchand. "And I want you to ensure that the Will is absolutely foolproof so that no one comes forward to lay a claim to my estate."

"And I can assure you that no one will be able to stake a claim to your grandson's inheritance. And that he and he alone shall be sole legal heir to your estate," Amarchand replied.

The Will was worded and drafted out as per Jagdeep's express specification as he would be leaving everything to his grandson. Amar would be sole heir to his grandfather's estate after his death as there would be no other claimants to Jagdeep's property. Jagdeep's only sibling was long dead, and as he did not wish to leave anything to his nieces, he had excluded them from his Will. Since they were kin who had not cared to keep in touch with their maternal uncle after the demise of their mother, Jagdeep was loath to include them as beneficiaries to his estate.

Jagdeep read through the contents of the Will, and he carefully scrutinized the legal document to ascertain that everything was in order before signing it. "Now, who will bear witness to this document? And who will testify to the authenticity of the Will?"

He asked Amarchand.

"Well, my Assistant, Rana Khanna, will do the honors." Amarchand stated, before asking his Assistant to sign as witness to Jagdeep's Will.

"The Will shall be kept in your custody until the day of its reading." Jagdeep handed over the legal document to his solicitor for safekeeping.

#

"Are you hungry, dadaji? Do you want to have lunch?" Amar asked Jagdeep once they had exited the solicitors' office. "I know just the place and its pretty close by too."

"Yes, that's not a bad idea. As a matter of fact, I'm starving, and could eat a horse right now," Jagdeep replied.

Amar drove to The Ambassador Hotel, and he handed the car keys to the valet to park the vehicle before entering the restaurant. The eatery was pretty crowded at this time of the afternoon, but in spite of the rush, the duo managed to get a table by the corner. And once they had occupied their seats, Amar signaled to the waiter to take their order.

The waiter strode to their table before handing them the menu card.

"Mutton biryani is the specialty here. And their kebabs are good too. You really should try it. And I'm sure you will like it."Amar suggested to Jagdeep.

"I'll go along with whatever you recommend since you know what's good here. And I'll leave it to you to place the order," Jagdeep said.

Amar turned to the waiter. "We will have two plates each of mutton biryani with sheekh kebabs. And two glasses of sweet lassi but without the ice. And can you make sure that there is absolutely no chilli in the food." He instructed, whilst ordering the meal.

"Yes, of course," the waiter affirmed before proceeding to the kitchen to relay their order.

Their food arrived shortly. And as they were both pretty hungry, they ravenously tucked into the meal, and they did not pause until they were sated and full.

"Dadaji, did you enjoy the food?"

Amar asked his grandfather once they had come to the end of their meal.

"Oh yes, I did. And we must come here more often as it is such a change from Rashmi's bland cooking which I can barely manage to eat," Jagdeep declared.

"You are well aware that Rashmi is only following doctor's orders. And it's for your own good, you know that," Amar said.

"That's a lot of baloney. And considering that my days are numbered and I don't have much longer to live, I should be allowed to eat what I want without any restrictions being imposed upon me," Jagdeep said. He was unhappy with the dietary restriction that was imposed upon him. And he hated being placed on an unpalatable diet of grilled, boiled vegetables bereft of any spices, which was his daily fare. Since food was his one great weakness, being told to watch what he ate was tantamount to being punished. And he wished to have a free hand in the choice of his daily menu.

"Stop grumbling about your diet dadaji since you are well aware that we only mean well." Amar gently chided Jagdeep for raising a protest over his dietary regimen.

"As I will not be around for very long, I think it's rather unfair to place any kind of restriction upon me. And I should not be put on a Spartan diet, but should be allowed to indulge in the foods I like while I still can," Jagdeep reiterated.

"Stop talking about your passing since you are well aware that the topic of your death upsets me," Amar said.

"Alright, I'm sorry if I upset you." Jagdeep apologized to Amar." I was just thinking aloud as it is inevitable," he said.

"You are forgiven." Amar accepted his grandfather's apology.

They settled the bill for the meal before stepping out of the restaurant arm-in-arm like comrades. And there was a warm camaraderie between the two which surpassed their disparate years.

Amar approached the valet. "Could you please bring the Blue Mercedes Benz?" He asked.

The valet soon brought their car. Jagdeep boarded the vehicle and sat in the front seat besides the driver whilst Amar took the wheel. And they fastened their seat belts before getting ready to leave the eatery.

They were about to drive out of the restaurant when Amar saw Rohit arrive. And he was in the company of a lady. As Rohit usually kept his Assistant informed about his business schedule, Amar was well aware of whom he met. Since Rohit had not mentioned anything about today's appointment, Amar was rather suspicious about the former's companion. And he wondered whether there was more to the lunch time meet than met the eye.

"Dadaji, guess who I just saw entering the restaurant?"

Amar addressed Jagdeep.

"I have no idea," Jagdeep replied.

"Nita's husband, Rohit, just drove up," Amar said.

"So what's the big deal?" Jagdeep asked. "He must have decided to have lunch outside of the office for a change."

"No, that's not what I meant?"

"Then, what exactly did you mean?" Jagdeep asked.

"I meant that Rohit was with a woman."

"Well, before you jump to any conclusions; she could be just about anyone. And for all you know, she must be a business acquaintance, and this is probably an official lunch," Jagdeep said.

"Yes, that's what I would have thought too. But Rohit usually keeps me informed about all his business appointments, and I don't remember him mentioning anything about today's meeting," Amar stated.

"Well then, perhaps it slipped his mind. Anyways I don't think you should make such a big deal out of it," Jagdeep remarked.

"I know Rohit well and it's not like him to forget, and especially when it comes to work. Somehow I cannot help getting the impression that this is not a regular business meeting," Amar said.

"And, what do you mean by that?" Jagdeep queried.

"I think Rohit is having an affair. And I am pretty certain that he is cheating on his wife," Amar replied.

"And what makes you so sure that Rohit is cheating on Nita?" Jagdeep asked. "Can you explain the grounds for your suspicion?"

"It's just my hunch," Amar reiterated.

"Then it's probably wrong. And even if it turns out to be true, there's nothing that you can do about it," Jagdeep retorted.

"Well if that's the case, Nita certainly deserves to know what her husband is up to behind her back," Amar declared.

"And who is going to bell the cat?" Jagdeep asked his grandson. "You are not Rohit's conscience keeper, and neither are you Nita's designated well-wisher since she has made it pretty clear that she wants nothing to do with you. And she didn't think twice before leading you on and breaking your heart. Take my advice and stay out of their private life. So far as you are concerned, Rohit is your boss and Nita is his wife. And don't ever forget that."

"Very well," Amar answered.

CHAPTER 20

Rohit met Meeta in an official capacity in the line of duty, and they hit it off very well from the start. They soon went from being mere business colleagues to become regular acquaintances. And they spent considerable time together. Meeta was a divorcee who was married briefly before her husband and she decided to part ways, and they divorced by mutual consent. And although they were long divorced, her ex-husband and she continued to keep in touch, and they remained good friends, while his present wife and children were rather fond of Meeta, and they treated her like family.

Rohit was presently with Meeta at the bistro, and they were having a casual chat over a cup of coffee.

"Meeta, I can't believe that I'm about to say this. But what do you say to the idea of having a friend with benefits?" Rohit asked. "I am referring to a physical relationship sans any binding ties purely to satiate the carnal needs. And you know what I mean by that? I hear that it's rather common these days."

"Do you mean the kind where one indulges in casual sex without any emotions involved?" Meeta queried.

"Yes, that's precisely what I meant; sex without the baggage of convention such as monogamy, matrimony, commitment and conservative notions of virtue, sinfulness and morality. And the physical act shall only be for pleasure. It appears to be the latest trend now-a-days."

"Well, I hope I don't come across as a nymphomaniac since I'm all game for such an arrangement as it will be fun. And as there are no emotions involved, we've nothing to lose," Meeta stated.

"I was afraid to moot the suggestion of casual sex since I feared you would strike down the idea, and would lash out at me for my immorality" Rohit said.

"I'm not a prude Rohit. And besides this is the 21st century and people are pretty broad-minded these days," Meeta reiterated.

"I want you to know that this arrangement is not binding in any way, and that we are not in a committed relationship of any sort. And that you are free to end it anytime you wish to," he said.

"Yes, of course, I'm aware that I can call it off anytime I want. And that's the reason why I agreed to the proposal in spite of it being rather unconventional," she averred.

"And, we are free to be with other people when we want. And no questions will be asked, and neither would any explanations be sought," Rohit reiterated.

"Yes, I understand," Meeta replied.

The arrangement suited the duo fine, and they did not find anything wrong with entering into a no-strings-attached relationship purely to satiate their carnal needs. And as there was no commitment from either side, they were not compelled to remain monogamous, and they were at liberty to bed others without being weighed down by the burden of guilt. Meeta refrained from bedding anyone else besides Rohit, but the latter, on the other hand, indulged in many one night stands. He brazenly admitted to being addicted to sex, and he sought to sate his carnal addiction.

#

Rohit had just returned to his office after attending a meeting when he received a text message from Meeta on his cell phone. And he could not help suppressing a smile when he read the message.

"Hi Rohit, how have you been? Could we meet over the weekend?" Meeta's text message read.

Though the content of the message was rather innocuous, Rohit was well aware of what Meeta meant. He knew that she was referring to a pleasure filled afternoon between the sheets when they indulged in satiating their physical needs.

Meeta's apartment was the chosen venue for their carnal trysts as it provided them with the privacy that they sought. Since she lived alone she was answerable to no one, and there were no prying eyes to be dealt with. As Meeta slipped naked into bed with Rohit, she eagerly looked forward to the pleasure filled afternoon. But even before she could commence her carnal antics, she received a series of texts on her cell phone.

"Ignore the messages; I'm sure they can wait. Or better still; switch off your phone so that no one can get through to you. Let's not ruin the afternoon." Rohit asked Meeta to pay no heed to the texts and he told her to desist from reading the messages.

"And believe me that's what I'd like to do, but this could be something very important." Meeta proceeded to check her cell phone. "I'm sorry Rohit, but I really do need to run out for a bit as it's rather urgent and just can't wait until later," she said.

"I won't pretend that I'm not disappointed but I know that it can't be helped; although the timing really sucks. I'll wait until you get back when we can make up for the lost time."

"Yes, I'll try my best to be back as soon as I can. And I promise I will make it up to you," Meeta averred. She soon got dressed, and left the apartment.

Rohit endeavored to keep himself busy in Meeta's absence, and he tried to while away the time until she returned. He switched on the television, and he tried to surf channels on the remote control, but no program appeared to interest him. Rohit was soon bored with watching the small screen, and he looked around for an alternative means of entertainment when he found a stack of fashion magazines lying on the table. He picked up the latest issue of VOGUE and casually flipped through the pages of the fashion magazine when he came across a familiar looking envelope. It was similar to the cover which he had received recently.

A second set of photographs were mailed to Rohit at his residence, and he had succeeded in destroying the racy snapshots before Nita could lay her eyes on them. As he had assumed that Ravi had sent the steamy pictures to him, Rohit had confronted the latter about the photos only to be met with a stout denial. And since learning that Ravi was not the sender of the latest set of pictures, Rohit had spent sleepless nights wondering who the anonymous blackmailer could be. He was now pretty certain that Meeta had mailed those pictures to him. And should she turn out to be the mysterious sender of the photographs, she was bound to have copies hidden in her apartment. Rohit decided to investigate, and he mulled searching the place for the telltale pictures. However, even before he could play sleuth and snoop around the apartment, Meeta returned home.

"I try my best not to take any work related calls on a weekend, but this, however, was unavoidable." Meeta attempted to offer an explanation for her unscheduled exit. And she was extremely apologetic for having left him unexpectedly. "Shall we make up for it now?"

"I'm not really in the mood now as the moment has passed," Rohit replied.

"Alright, I understand. And I'm equally disappointed too," Meeta stated.

"Was there any major problem though considering your hurried exit?"

Rohit asked Meeta.

"Well, although it was an emergency, there certainly was no fire anywhere," Meeta quipped. "Our afternoon, however, went awry though."

"Yes, and that's a real shame," Rohit averred.

"Well, I see that you've kept yourself busy while I was away. And I had no idea that you were into fashion," Meeta remarked, when she saw Rohit with the copy of the VOGUE in his hand.

"Oh no, it's nothing of the sort; I just happened to pick up the first magazine that I saw, and was trying to kill time until you got back." Rohit answered. "By the way, I found this envelope between the pages. Where did you get this from?" He asked, displaying the cover that he had come across in the fashion magazine.

"I borrowed a few when I ran out of covers," Meeta answered.

"And who did you borrow these from?" Rohit queried.

"I don't quite recollect."

"Can you at least try to remember where you got these covers from?" He reiterated

"And why does it matter where they came from? And why is it so important for you to know the origin of this envelope?"

Meeta asked Rohit.

"No, it isn't. And forget that I even asked," Rohit replied.

CHAPTER 21

Amar was set up on a blind date by his friend, Manu, with a distant cousin. And although he was loath to get acquainted with the latter's cousin, Manu, however, succeeded in convincing him to meet his date.

"Just how long are you going to mope for Nita?' Manu asked Amar. "It's high time you forgot her and tried to find love again."

"I don't know if I'm ready to enter the dating scene just yet," Amar averred.

"Well, you could meet Gia, and decide for yourself whether you wish to take the relationship forward."

"Should I decide against pursuing the relationship, will it affect our friendship in any way? And would we end up falling out with each other?"

"Goodness no, that's being very petty and small-minded."

"Alright then, just where do I meet up with your cousin?"

Amar asked Manu.

"I've arranged for you to meet Gia at the lobby of The Oberoi Hotel around 5.00 P.M. today," Manu said.

"And how would I recognize Gia considering I've never seen her before?" Amar queried.

"Well, Gia is very fair with auburn coloured shoulder length hair, and she has large hazel eyes. She will be wearing a blue polka dotted dress, and she will be carrying a black Dior handbag. You won't miss her," Manu averred.

"I certainly hope so as it would be rather awkward should I go up to the wrong person and introduce myself as her date for the evening," Amar said. " By the way, is Gia tall or short?"

"Gia is of average height, and she generally wears three inch platform heels. Anyways, you have her cell number should there be any confusion. And let me know how the date went."

#

Amar reached The Oberoi Hotel shortly after 5.00 P.M., and after parking the car at the parking lot, he entered the hotel. He looked around the lobby for a girl who fit Gia's description before he spotted her.

Gia was seated at a table by the corner, and she was sipping coffee.

Amar proceeded towards Gia. "Hi, I am Amar, and I'm your date for the evening." He introduced himself to her.

"And I am Gia," she replied.

"Do you mind if I join you?"

Amar asked Gia.

"No, not at all. Go ahead." Gia invited Amar to the table.

"To be very honest; I was rather reluctant to agree to this date and had to be coaxed into coming here. And I hope you don't think I'm being rude," he said.

"I appreciate the candor, and to tell you the truth, I wasn't inclined to meet you either. And it took a lot of persuasion on Manu's part before I finally agreed to this blind date," Gia replied.

"I know that Manu only has the best interest at heart and he wants us to fall in love, but frankly I don't see that happening as I am still nursing a broken heart," Amar stated.

"And as for me, I'm still grieving for my dead fiancé," she replied.

"I am sorry to hear about your fiancé. How did he die?"

Amar asked Gia.

"Rishabh plunged to his death from a cliff while he was out on a picnic with friends."

"That's terrible indeed. And that must've been a great shock."

"Yes, it was. And it happened just days before the wedding."

"That's very tragic."

"Well, I've gotten over it now. But I'm just not ready to start dating again," Gia said.

"I can understand how you feel. And now that we're clear as to where we stand, I presume there will be no expectations from either side, and that a romance will not brew between us," Amar said.

"Yes, absolutely," Gia affirmed.

Once they were completely honest with each other and succeeded in dispelling any wrong notions that they might have had; the duo connected instantly. They struck up a friendship before the evening was through, and they laid the foundation for a long lasting association.

"Tell me about yourself."

Amar asked Gia about her family.

"Well, my father is a retired corporate head who now leads a life of leisure, and he divides his time between our holiday home in Alibaug and our residence in Mumbai. And my mother is a fashion designer who runs a high-end boutique at the Taj Lands End, at Bandra. While my parents reside at the family home at Bandra, I've taken up an apartment on rent at Churchgate as it's closer to my place of work."

"Well, as for me, I live with my grandfather. And he is the only family I have," Amar stated.

Amar and Gia soon became the best of friends, and she could not have asked for a better friend in her life. Gia turned to Amar when she needed help of any sort, and he would set everything aside to be there by her side.

Amar took Gia home to meet his grandfather. "Dadaji, this is my friend, Gia." He introduced her to Jagdeep.

"I'm pleased to finally meet you. I've heard so much about you, and my grandson has told me what a wonderful friend you are," Jagdeep stated.

"Well it's mutual, since I couldn't have asked for a better friend than Amar," Gia replied.

#

Jagdeep took an instant liking to Gia, and his fondness for her grew over time. He found her to be warm and genuine, and he was not averse to the idea of having her as family.

"I think Gia is a wonderful person. And I appear to have grown rather fond of her," Jagdeep told his grandson one fine day.

"And that's the reason why she is my friend," Amar answered.

"Have you thought of moving this friendship forward?" Jagdeep asked.

"And what do you mean?" Amar queried.

"Have you thought of considering Gia as more than just a friend?" Jagdeep reiterated.

"No dadaji, absolutely not, and don't you start getting any ideas," Amar stated.

"And why aren't you willing to consider Gia in a different light?" Jagdeep asked Amar. "After all, she has all the qualities to make a good wife."

"That's because I have never looked at Gia in that manner."

"Well then it's time you saw Gia in a different light as you should now think of getting married and starting a family. After all, you're not getting any younger," Jagdeep stated.

"I will settle down to a married life when the time is right," Amar reiterated.

"I missed out on the growing years of my son as I was too busy trying to make money. And I'd now like to see my son live his childhood through his grandchildren," Jagdeep said.

"And you will, I promise, but there's still time for that," Amar averred.

"Is Nita the reason why you don't want to consider marrying Gia?" Jagdeep queried. "And if that's the case, you're wasting your time, since Nita has made it pretty clear that she wants to be with her husband."

"It's silly of you to ask me whether Nita is the reason why I cannot consider marriage since you are well aware that we can never be together. The reason why I cannot consider marrying Gia is because I don't love her, and I can't ever imagine falling in love with her. Gia is just a good friend and nothing more," Amar averred.

CHAPTER 22

Rohit was at the dance bar with his friend, Arjun, and the duo was watching a group of garishly clad girls setting the dance floor on fire. The dancers were gyrating to the tune of loud Hindi film songs which was being played in the background. And as they swayed seductively to the rhythm of the music, crisp one hundred rupee bills rained down upon them. The patrons were more than magnanimous in their appreciation of the performers, and they generously showered the dancers with money.

The dance performance continued into the wee hours of the morning, and it was well-nigh the crack of dawn when the girls finally stopped entertaining their audience. And by then it was time to vacate the place.

"It's pretty late, and I should be getting home now. My wife will probably be wondering where I am," Arjun said.

"Well, you can leave if you wish, but I would like to stay back," Rohit stated.

"And why would you want to stay back when this place is shutting down for the night?" Arjun asked.

"I have my reasons," Rohit replied.

"Alright then, it's up to you to stay. As for me, I am leaving now. Goodnight." Arjun bid Rohit adieu before departing from the venue. And he left to return home.

Rohit sought out the manager soon after Arjun had left the place. "I wish to have a girl." He expressed his desire to have a companion for the night.

"Well, before I agree to your demand, I should make it very clear that our girls don't come cheap. And you will be required to pay a steep price to bed a girl for the night," the manager said.

"Yes, I'm well aware that your girls are rather pricey, and I am willing to pay the price that's asked of me," Rohit replied.

"And I also want to make it clear that the girls don't indulge in sadomasochism of any kind since that's an absolute no. And there will be no unnatural sex either if you know what I mean," the manager stated.

"I can assure you that I won't indulge in anything of the sort. There will be no sadomasochism or any kind of kinky sex," Rohit affirmed.

"And I expect you to adhere to the rules or else you will be heavily penalized."

"Absolutely," Rohit averred.

The manager escorted Rohit to a room at the rear of the bar where over a dozen girls were flocked. "These are the girls who are available for the night. And you can have your pick." He asked Rohit to choose his pick from amongst the assembled women.

Rohit carefully surveyed the girls before he finally zeroed in on one. "I'd like to have the third girl from the right," he said.

"Tina. Her name is Tina."

Tina was rather petite with delicate features and large luminous eyes that seemed to dominate her tiny heart shaped face. She was honey hued with lush jet black hair that fell gently upon her shoulder. And she appeared to be of good breeding.

Tina led Rohit to a large cubicle which could be latched from the inside so as to provide them with privacy. And the compartment was comfortably furnished with a large luxurious double bed that had ample room for two.

"What's a decent guy like you doing in a place like this?" Tina asked Rohit. "You don't come across as the sort who frequents dance bars."

"And believe me, I don't. My friend and I came here for the very first time today out of sheer curiosity just to see what this place was all about. And as I was told that the girls here were adept at pleasuring a man, I decided to see for myself whether it was really true," Rohit replied.

"I hope this is the first and the last time that you visit this place as I don't wish to see you here again. Men of your ilk shouldn't be seen at this sleazy joint as it does your reputation no good," Tina said.

"And I don't wish to come here ever again after tonight," Rohit averred." By the way; the same goes for you too. You don't strike me as being a typical bar dancer. So what's a girl like you doing at this place? And how did you end up dancing at a bar?"

"Well, to cut a long story short; I decided to eke out a living dancing at the bar to get away from my stepfather who turned into a savage brute after my mother's passing. And I don't need your sympathy as I've seen far worse before I came here, and my life in this place is not all that bad when compared to the hell I called home," Tina stated. "We've wasted far too much time talking, and I'd like to get down to business now." She reminded Rohit about the purpose of this meet.

"Yes, of course."

Rohit soon disrobed, and he commenced his carnal antics. And Tina did not disappoint him since she was well worth the price that he had paid for her. Although he vowed that he would not set foot inside the dance bar again after tonight, Rohit knew that it would be a difficult promise for him to keep.

Tina soon became an addiction with Rohit, and he sought her out night after night to satiate his carnal needs. He stopped by at the dance bar every evening after work before returning home, and it became a daily routine with him. Rohit indulged Tina by giving her innumerable gifts, and before long, he established a special bond with her.

CHAPTER 23

Rohit had just entered the office and he looked around the room to ensure that everything was in order, and that nothing had been displaced. And it was a habit which he had developed since the photographs had vanished from his custody. He was pleased to note that nothing seemed to be out of place, but despite the orderliness of the room, he, however, got the impression that someone had been near the safe. And he sought to confirm his suspicion. Although, he no longer kept anything personal at the work place ever since the photographs had disappeared, the office cabinet, however, contained very important documents; some of which were highly confidential. And Rohit wanted to ensure that those documents had not fallen into the wrong hands.

He was astounded by the sight that he saw when he opened the safe. The photographs which had vanished earlier from his custody were now back in its original place. And whosoever had taken the pictures had not gone through the trouble of placing them in a cover, as they appeared to have made a hasty retreat before their crime could be discovered. Now that the photographs were back with him, Rohit hoped that his troubles were all over. And that he would no longer be subjected to any angst or fear every time a similar looking cover arrived for him in the mail.

It would be foolish to leave the photographs in the office as he could never tell what would happen next. And neither could he hazard a guess as to who else would lay their eyes on the steamy pictures, and be privy to his dirty secret. Rohit wished to have that dark chapter of his life buried and forgotten, and he never wanted to go down that path again. And as the racy photographs would be a constant reminder of the times that he wished to forget, he wanted to obliterate all trace of those telltale snapshots before it could do him any more harm. He carefully ran the pictures through the shredder, and he shredded them to bits, before putting a light to it. He set the shredded pictures alight with a cigarette lighter, and he watched them burn and turn to soot before discarding the blackened soot in the waste basket in the room.

Rohit had barely settled down at his desk after completing the task when Raveena entered the room.

"You have an appointment with the dentist at 4.30 P.M. today". Raveena reminded Rohit about the dental appointment that was scheduled for later in the day.

"Thank you for reminding me about the appointment as it had completely slipped my mind," Rohit stated. He had managed to get an appointment with the dentist after much difficulty. As his infected root canal was causing him a great deal of pain, he had requested for an urgent appointment, and Dr. Modi was kind enough to reschedule his other patients in order to oblige Rohit.

Since he did not want to miss out on his doctor's appointment, Rohit left early from work. He had a word with Amar before leaving the office, and he issued last minute instructions to his Assistant. "Amar, I would like an e-mail to be sent to all concerned about the meeting that is scheduled in my office on Monday morning at 11.00 A.M. And kindly ensure that the agenda is sent out before the end of the day so that everyone comes prepared." Rohit said to his Assistant.

"Very well, and it shall be done," Amar affirmed.

#

Dr. Haren Modi was a reputed dental surgeon whose clinic was situated in Dental House at Kemps Corner. As his appointment diary was generally chock-a-block with appointments, and he usually had a very tight schedule, he was compelled to make some adjustments in his busy schedule in order to accommodate Rohit.

Rohit arrived at the dental clinic shortly before 4.00 P.M., and he was asked to wait at the reception until he was shown inside.

Dr. Modi administered Rohit a dose of anesthesia before commencing the root canal. And Rohit was spared the agony of pain and discomfort during the dental procedure.

"The root canal was painless on account of the anesthesia that was administered to you, but you will, however, be in a considerable amount of pain once the anesthesia wears off. I have prescribed some painkillers for you to take," Dr. Modi stated, once he had ended the dental procedure.

"Very well, and I shall procure the pills right away," Rohit replied.

Rohit stopped by at the drug store next door and bought the painkillers before proceeding home. He was just entering his apartment building when he received a voicemail from Meeta on his cell phone.

"Hi Rohit, how have you been? I've not seen you in a while. Could we meet over the weekend as it's rather urgent? And call me once you get this message. I will be waiting to hear from you," Meeta's voicemail stated.

"I have just returned from the dentist after a painful root canal, and will be unable to make it over the weekend, but we could meet on Monday evening at the Starbucks coffee shop."

Rohit sent Meeta a text message in reply to her voicemail. And he agreed to see her on Monday after work instead of meeting her over the weekend.

#

Rohit left immediately after work to keep his rendezvous with Meeta. But when he reached the coffee shop, he found that she had not yet arrived, and he was kept waiting.

Meeta showed up shortly. And she was profusely apologetic for having turned up late. "I am so sorry to have kept you waiting but it just couldn't be helped. My car had a puncture, and I had to have the vehicle towed to the nearest garage before I could take a cab to get here." She elucidated the reason for her delay.

"Car trouble can be really inconvenient, and that too when you least expect it," Rohit said.

"Yes, I know. Anyways, I am planning to sell the vehicle shortly provided I get a good price. By the way, I was really disappointed at not seeing you over the weekend as I had looked forward to our time together. And it's been so long since our carnal tryst," Meeta said.

"I'm sorry that I let you down. But as I was in a great deal of pain after the dental procedure, I decided to stay put at home over the weekend. And our capering was the last thing on my mind," Rohit replied.

"Yes, I know the agony of a root canal since I've been through it too, and it can be pretty painful. I hope you are much better now."

Meeta enquired about Rohit's well-being post the dental procedure.

"Yes, I'm fine now. And thank you for asking. By the way, what was the urgency all about?" He asked.

"Nothing of much consequence really, but I was rather concerned as I had not heard from you in a while. And I was worried that something was wrong with you," Meeta replied.

"I am afraid I've been rather tied up lately. And that has left me with no time for anything else," Rohit said.

"Well, I find that quite strange as it was never the case before. And no matter how busy you were, you always managed to find the time for us. Is there something that you're not telling me here?"

Meeta asked Rohit.

"Well, since I don't wish to lie, I will be very frank and honest. And I hope you understand. I feel the time has come for us to put an end to our casual relationship," Rohit stated.

"And what do you mean by that?" Meeta asked.

"I mean to say that it's time for us to stop being friends with benefits since staleness has now crept into this relationship. And this arrangement no longer holds any thrill for me and neither does it excite me any longer," Rohit reiterated.

Tina now satiated Rohit's carnal needs, and she transported him to the pinnacles of ecstasy. And he no longer required Meeta to fulfill his erotic demands.

"Well, I know that our relationship was very casual and that it was purely physical. And that there was no commitment or emotions involved from either side. And nor was there any exclusivity. However, you must admit that we had a good thing going, and that it was an enjoyable pastime," Meeta averred.

"Yes, I know that we had our moments. And it was fun while it lasted but not anymore, I am afraid. As boredom has crept into this relationship, the time has now come for us to look elsewhere to satisfy our physical needs," Rohit said.

"Do you mean to say that you've gotten bored with me? And that you no longer have any use for me?" She asked.

"Well, in a manner of speaking, that's precisely what I meant. Besides, you are well aware of the nature of this relationship, aren't you?" He reiterated.

"I certainly have no illusions, and I know where I stand," Meeta declared.

It was no secret that theirs was a physical relationship which began and ended in bed, and that there were no emotions involved. And it was a given that they were two people who hopped into bed when the need arose and went their separate ways once their carnal needs were fulfilled.

"Then you will agree with me when I say that it is time to call off our arrangement which in any case was not binding on either side. And we could go back to being acquaintances without the casual sex," Rohit stated.

"I'm sorry but that's not your decision alone to make. It was a joint decision to agree to this arrangement and we'll end it when I am ready. And I'm not ready to end our casual relationship just yet," Meeta retorted.

"It's too bad you should feel that way, because so far as I am concerned, I'm no longer your bedfellow. And you will have to look for someone else to pleasure you between the sheets from now onwards," Rohit stated, before rising to leave. And he departed from the coffee shop without waiting for Meeta to furnish her reply.

CHAPTER 24

A parcel was hand delivered to Rohit at his residence, and although the sender's name was missing, he was pretty certain that the package had come from Arjun. Rohit had asked Arjun to send a volume of encyclopedias to his residence, and he was awaiting the arrival of the same. However, when he opened the package he discovered that the parcel did not contain the encyclopedias which he was expecting, and he was rather surprised by the contents. The racy pictures had managed to surface once more, and the steamy photographs of him and Rahul together were sent to him yet again. And Rohit wondered how these photographs had managed to surface in spite of him having gone through great lengths to destroy them.

#

Meeta was not surprised to hear from Rohit as she had been expecting his call. And she knew that it was only a matter of time before he got in touch with her.

"Hello, Rohit, and how have you been? I didn't quite expect to hear from you again considering the way you walked out on me the other day." Meeta mocked Rohit. And she feigned to be surprised to hear from him.

"Don't you try to be smart with me since I know what you're up to," Rohit replied.

"Alright, I won't pretend I wasn't expecting your call. In fact, I was wondering when I'd hear from you and would've been very surprised had you chosen to remain silent," Meeta said.

"Just what the hell do you think you're doing?"

Rohit asked Meeta.

"And what do you mean?" Meeta asked.

"You know very well what I mean?" Rohit reiterated. "And stop pretending you don't know what I'm talking about. I am referring to the photographs of Rahul and me together which you sent across to my residence," he thundered. Rohit was seething with rage, and he would have gladly wrung Meeta's neck and snuffed out her life that very instant if he could.

"Well, the two of you certainly do make a cute couple, don't you think? And I'm sure the others would see it that way too," Meeta stated.

"Don't you dare even think about going public with the pictures? You'll live to regret it. And I promise you will be sorry."

Rohit threatened Meeta with dire consequences should she attempt to go public with the steamy pictures. And despite dreading the very thought of his worst kept secret being put out in the public domain, he endeavored to put up a brave front. He did not want Meeta to know that he feared the consequences of the pictures being put on display. And he did not want her to have the faintest idea that he was terrified of being exposed.

"You better listen to me first Rohit. I am not afraid of you and you can't intimidate me with your empty threats. And neither can you stop me from displaying the pictures for everyone to see. In fact, there's nothing that you can do about it," Meeta replied. She was unfazed by Rohit's threat since she could see through his bluff, and she sensed his fear at being exposed. And she knew that he was in dread of his dirty secret being brought out into the open.

"Did you send me the photographs earlier too? And were you the one behind the phone calls subsequent to the delivery of the pictures?"

Rohit asked Meeta whether she was the sender of the earlier set of photographs which he had accused Ravi of mailing him. And he asked her whether she was behind the string of anonymous phone calls which he had received subsequent to the arrival of the snapshots.

"Don't be ridiculous. That wasn't me. I got these pictures only two days ago. However, I must warn you that there are more where these came from. Besides, I've made sufficient copies too," Meeta declared. "And as for the intimidating phone calls; I have no idea what you're talking about," she averred.

"How did you get these photos, anyway?"

Rohit asked Meeta.

"I'm not about to tell you that. Anyways, does it really matter?" Meeta asked.

"Yes, it matters to me," Rohit reiterated.

"Well, I'm afraid that's a long story."

"And I'm willing to listen."

"Well, I don't feel inclined to satisfy your curiosity. And you can keep wondering how I got the photos," Meeta said.

"Is it what I think it is?"

"Yes, you're absolutely right," she averred.

"Are you trying to blackmail me?" Rohit queried.

"You are at liberty to assume what you like. These pictures will go viral. And they will be uploaded on the website for the world to see," she said.

"You wouldn't dare do that."

"Watch me. Anyways, you can rest assured that no one has seen these pictures as yet. And I guarantee you that no one will ever lay their eyes on the photos provided you agree to my demand."

"And what do you want from me?"

Rohit asked Meeta.

"Ten Crores and nothing less," Meeta said.

"You are out of your mind," he exclaimed

"That's what it'll take for me to back off," she reiterated.

"That's a lot of money you're talking about," Rohit said.

"That's my price. Take it or leave it. It's entirely up to you," Meeta retorted.

"But you are well aware that I don't have that kind of money. And it's like asking for the moon," he said.

"Then, that's your problem, not mine." She answered.

"And what happens if I don't agree to pay you the ten Crores?" Rohit asked.

"Then you know what the consequences will be," Meeta said. She was well aware that Rohit did not have the kind of money which she had demanded, but she expected him to come up with the amount all the same. She wanted Rohit to resort to whatever means possible to fulfill her demand, and failing which his dirty secret would be privy to the cyber world. Meeta was pretty sure that the racy pictures would cause quite a sensation as Rohit Kumar was well known in the corporate circle. And the raunchy images of him cavorting with his superior would be viewed with much glee.

CHAPTER 25

Meeta was setting out to visit her mother at the Retirement Home in Pune. And though she usually took the Deccan Queen or rode by the VOLVO bus to get to the city, she, however, decided to drive down to Pune today instead of opting for the public transport. As she had bought herself a new pair of wheels, she did not anticipate any car trouble en route, and since it was a Sunday, she did not expect much traffic on the Expressway. And she presumed that it would be a pleasurable drive.

She stopped by at the gas station before embarking upon her journey. "I want the fuel tank to be filled to full capacity." Meeta instructed the petrol pump attendant.

Once she had filled the car tank with fuel, she gave the automobile a quick look over, and she inspected the vehicle briefly before commencing upon her journey.

The weather was pleasant, and it was an ideal day for a long drive. Meeta rolled down the car window to enjoy the cool breeze.

#

Roses Retirement Home was spread over a few acres, and its residents were mostly the elderly and the aged whose children were busy with their own lives. And though their children did not love them any less, they were, however, unable to devote sufficient time to their parents as their priorities had since changed. Under the circumstances, the elderly parents opted to reside in a community home rather than live on their own. As there was sufficient company at the Retirement Home, they were never lonely, and some had even managed to make friends. Apart from the company that community living provided them, all their needs were also taken care of for them.

The Retirement Home gave the members of the 60-and-over club a luxurious lifestyle that younger folks would envy. The home came complete with elegant interiors, gourmet meals, modern gymnasiums with personal trainers and a club house. Moreover, they did not have to worry about leaking faucets, paying electricity bills, or even cooking and doing the laundry, if they did not want to. That was all taken care of for the residents. There was even a concierge to arrange transport and tickets, and guest suites for visitors.

The recreational facility at the Retirement Home left little or no time for boredom. The community boasted of an exhaustive activity list; everything ranging from concerts to pottery classes. The residents were happy and content with the kind of life they led away from their children.

Meeta reached the Retirement Home shortly before noon.

"I'm really glad to see you. I missed you, you know," Meeta's mother, Mohini, said, when she arrived.

Mohini was delighted to see Meeta. She eagerly looked forward to her daughter's visits, and she missed the latter when she was away. And though there were times she wished Meeta lived with her, Mohini; however, never let her daughter know that she was unhappy without her since she did not want Meeta to be wracked with guilt for wanting to lead her own life.

"I'm sorry I could not come to see you last month as I was rather tied up and couldn't find the time." Meeta apologized to her mother for skipping the usual visit schedule the previous month.

"That's okay and I understand that it's difficult for you to get away sometimes. And I know that you are a very busy person. So stop going down a guilt trip for being unable to spare the time for me," Mohini replied.

"Well mamma, how have you been?"

Meeta asked Mohini.

"I'm getting on fine and doing rather well for my age. You, on the other hand, look thinner each time I see you. And you are now beginning to look like a bag of bones. Have you not been eating well? Or are you on a diet, as usual?"

Mohini asked Meeta.

"I'm just trying to maintain my figure. And you know how it is these days. No one wants to be fat," Meeta said.

"You mean to say that you are starving yourself to remain fashionably thin?" Mohini asked. "You're beginning to look malnourished," she remarked.

"Mamma, that's an exaggeration; and you know it. The truth is that I'm eating less," Meeta reiterated.

"I can never understand your obsession to remain thin. And thin is not beautiful, you know," Mohini sighed.

"Well, then don't even try to see it my way. Anyways don't make it sound quite as dramatic since I am absolutely fine," Meeta said.

As they were meeting after a fairly long time, both mother and daughter had plenty to say to each other. Meeta had no secrets from Mohini and she told her mother just about everything that was going on in her life. And there was nothing that Meeta hid from Mohini; irrespective of whether her mother approved of it or not. Mohini was aware of Meeta's casual sexual relationship with Rohit, and as she belonged to the old school, she did not approve of a carnal relationship sans the emotions. According to Mohini, a relationship that was primarily for physical pleasure amounted to sacrilege of the body, and that, in her opinion, was unethical and immoral.

"Mamma, you will be pleased to know that Rohit and I have decided to call off our arrangement, and we are no longer in a casual sexual relationship," Meeta said.

"Well, I'm glad that you finally saw some sense and decided to end a relationship which had no future. I never approved of Rohit anyways as I have no respect for a man who cheats on his wife. And shame on Rohit for being unfaithful to the woman he married," Mohini stated.

"Mamma, please look around, and you'll see that people are cheating in their respective relationships. And it's a common occurrence these days," Meeta averred.

"Well, it certainly didn't happen in our days as only people of loose morals had a fling outside of marriage. And marriage was sacrosanct and expected to be revered," Mohini replied.

"I'm afraid that's not the case anymore. Marriage is no longer a deterrent to indulge in a little fun, and people do it all the time," Meeta stated.

"I must say that I'm appalled by today's generation. They don't seem to have any values," Mohini exclaimed.

"You lived in the Stone Age, mamma. This is the modern day and age," Meeta reiterated.

"Nonsense, you can be modern without being promiscuous," Mohini shot back.

Meeta rolled her eyes in disbelief at Mohini's statement. Her mother was out of touch with the times, and it was futile to try and reason with her by telling her that infidelity was accepted in today's world. Meeta felt it would be far wiser to change the topic before her mother embarked upon a long winded moral lecture which she had heard innumerable times before. She usually turned a deaf ear to her mother's sermons which invariably went in through one ear and out through the other without so much as even registering. Mohini was wasting her breath lecturing to her daughter as Meeta never ever heeded her advice.

"The last time I was here you mentioned about getting your cataract operated. Have you finally decided upon the laser?"

Meeta asked Mohini about the eye surgery which she was slated to undergo. As Mohini's cataract was in the very initial stage, she was advised to undergo a simple laser surgery to rid her of the problem. And she was told to have the procedure done as early as possible.

"I've decided not to have the surgery immediately. And will probably have the procedure done after a couple of months," Mohini replied.

"Well, don't postpone the surgery until too late as the sooner you get the cataract operated the better. Anyways, when you decide to have the procedure, do let me know well in advance so that I can be there with you," Meeta stated. As she would be required to take time off from her busy schedule to accompany her mother to the surgery, she would have to be given prior notice to keep those dates free. And since Mohini would require special care post the eye surgery, she would stay with her daughter until the time she was in a position to move back to the Retirement Home.

"Yes, of course. I'll give you sufficient notice so that you can take time off to be with me," Mohini averred.

#

Meeta had tea with her mother before leaving.

Mohini had made her daughter her favorite carrot halwa, and she piled Meeta's plate with a generous helping of the sweet.

"Mamma, that's too large a piece of halwa. And I'm afraid I won't be able to finish it," Meeta stated, when she saw the portion of the sweetmeat that she was served.

"I've gone through so much trouble to make this sweet dish especially for you. The least you can do is to eat the halwa without making a fuss. Forget about dieting for a day." Mohini chided her daughter for being fussy.

Meeta soon took leave of Mohini. "Alright mamma, you take care until I see you next. I will be back again the next month." She bid her mother adieu with a promise to visit her the following month.

Mohini hugged Meeta warmly. "Be cautious whilst on the road. Traffic can be very treacherous sometimes. Reach home safely."

"Yes, mamma, I promise I will be a careful driver. You take care of yourself. And I'll look forward to seeing you next month."

Meeta kissed Mohini lightly on the cheek before departing.

#

Meeta took a leisurely drive back as she was in no hurry to reach home, and she listened to the radio in the car while she drove. She heard some of her favorite songs being played, and she hummed along with Frank and Nancy Sinatra as they sang "Strangers in the Night".

There was not much traffic on the expressway, and the highway was more or less empty except for an occasional car or two which drove past Meeta and sped away. Hers was the only vehicle for miles on end until a truck overtook her and sped ahead before taking a complete u-turn and driving back towards her. The trucker and she were now on a collision course as they were heading towards each other.

Meeta tried to draw the trucker's attention to let him know that he was on the wrong side. She waved frantically to the truck driver, and she blew the horn continuously in a bid to get his attention, but all her attempts to get the trucker to notice her proved to be in vain. The trucker did not try to turn around and neither did he attempt to reverse the vehicle; instead he continued to hurtle towards her at breakneck speed. The truck was drawing closer as it covered the distance between them, and the trucker was gradually inching towards Meeta. And before long, he would collide with her car. The monstrous vehicle racing towards Meeta reminded her of the Grim Reaper, and she realized that she was staring into the face of death. And she wanted to get down from the car before it was too late.

She killed the engine, and she brought the car to a grinding halt before unfastening the seat belt and opening the door. However, even before she could step out of the car and abandon the automobile, the truck made contact with her vehicle, and it was soon over. The truck collided head-on with Meeta's Mini Cooper and crushed the car instantly. And the severe impact of the collision reduced her vehicle to a mangled heap of metal.

Meeta involuntarily shut her eyes when the truck collided with her car, and her lips moved in a silent prayer. Mercifully for her; death was instantaneous, and she felt no pain.

CHAPTER 26

Rohit was on taut tenterhooks and he was a nervous wreck while he waited for Ali to show up at the Marine Drive Promenade. And when Ali did not reach the venue at the designated time, he could not help but fear the worst, as he was afraid that things had gone awry and that their mission had failed.

Ali, however, arrived an hour later than the appointed time, and he turned up inordinately late for their meeting.

"I was beginning to get really worried, and I thought perhaps something had gone terribly wrong when you failed to show up earlier," Rohit stated.

"I'm sorry to have kept you waiting for over an hour, but since you specifically told me to make myself invisible; I had to take all the necessary precautions to ensure that I was not being followed on my way here." Ali stated, and he apologized for his late arrival which he attributed to Rohit's instructions.

"You don't have to apologize for being late as that's not what I'm worried about. All I am concerned about is the outcome of the mission. Did everything go as per our plan? And was it executed successfully?"

Rohit asked Ali.

"You can rest assured that all went well, and that everything was perfectly executed. And you have no more cause for any worry. Meeta is dead. She was killed in the collision between my truck and her car. And no one will ever suspect or for that matter; even have the faintest inkling that the fatal accident was a staged affair," Ali answered.

Rohit had sought Ali's help to eliminate Meeta in a bid to prevent her from spilling his dirty secret onto the public domain. And Ali suggested an orchestrated accident at the time. The staged automobile collision was Ali's idea as the fatal car crash would never be attributed to Rohit, and the latter would not be blamed for Meeta's death. Meeta's death would be dismissed as a road accident with her falling yet another victim to a rogue vehicle, and Rohit would get away with cold-blooded murder.

"Are you absolutely certain that we will get away with the automobile accident? And that no one will ever suspect that the fatal car crash was staged? Is our plan absolutely foolproof?"

Rohit asked Ali.

"I'm positive. The horrific collision will be dismissed as just another road accident which occurs every other day. And anyways everyone knows that Indian highways are virtual death traps, and that you take the road at your own risk." Ali stated; and he sought to allay Rohit's fears.

"Are you quite certain that you've not left behind any clues that could lead back to us?" Rohit queried. "I don't want the authorities arriving at my doorstep to investigate the accident, and pinning Meeta's death to me," he said.

"Well, you have nothing to fear since I took the utmost precaution to ensure that no fingers would be pointed towards us. Firstly, the truck was stolen from the dump yard so there would be no record of the vehicle, and I took care to change the number plates. And as the number plates were false, it would not be traced. I made sure that I didn't leave behind any fingerprints since I had worn gloves, and the shoe size too would not match mine as I had worn sneakers which were a foot size larger than mine; all with the intention of fooling the investigators. And it would be virtually impossible for anyone to zero in on the killer driver," Ali declared.

"Did anyone see you leaving the scene after the accident? And were there any witnesses who saw you fleeing from the site of the crash?"

Rohit asked Ali.

"No one saw me leave the scene of the accident as I took adequate care of that as well. I managed to jump out of the speeding truck minutes before it collided with Meeta's car, and I got away from the site of the car crash as quickly as I could. I don't think I've run as fast in my life. I vanished from the scene almost in an instant without drawing any attention to myself. And no one will ever suspect the collision to be anything other than an accident," Ali reiterated.

"That's good. And now that we've managed to successfully carry out the bloody mission, I'd advise you to disappear for a few days. And it would be better for you to fall off the grid until the accident investigation runs cold and all leads are lost. And I'd like you to go underground for the next couple of days," Rohit stated.

"Well, that would be rather difficult as there are only so many places where I could hide without being found," Ali answered.

"Not if you leave the city? And I mean tonight."

"I am afraid that's not possible at such short notice," Ali said.

"Not once you have the tickets in hand," Rohit averred.

"And what do you mean?"

Ali asked Rohit.

"I have arranged for you to travel to your hometown tonight, and you'll be leaving for Bihar by this evening's train. I'm sure you must be looking forward to seeing your family."

Rohit handed Ali the rail ticket for his journey later that evening, and the latter was given confirmed tickets to travel to Patna that same night.

"This is reward enough for all the trouble that I have been through. And I couldn't thank you enough for arranging for me to visit Patna as I've wanted to see my family for some time," Ali said. He was delighted to travel to Patna. As his wife and children resided with his parents in his home town, he was glad to avail of the opportunity to meet them.

#

Rohit left for Meeta's apartment shortly after his meeting with Ali, and he let himself into her home with the spare key that was kept hidden under the flower pot at the entrance. He did a thorough search of the apartment, and he went through the place with a fine-tooth comb until he found what he was looking for. He stumbled upon the telltale photographs under the mattress, and he found the steamy pictures well hidden in Meeta's bed. Rohit took the snapshots with him before leaving the apartment as he wished to destroy them once he returned home. He blamed Rahul for all his troubles since it was he who had insisted upon them being filmed together on his Polaroid purely on a whim. And Rahul's impulsiveness had led to his cup of woes. With the photographs back in his possession, Rohit hoped that his troubles were finally over.

He had barely finished breakfast the following morning when Meeta's ex-husband, Gurudev, showed up at the apartment. "Hello Gurudev, this is a pleasant surprise indeed. I didn't expect you here at this time of the day," Rohit said.

"I'm sorry to have dropped in unannounced like this but I had to see you urgently." Gurudev apologized to Rohit for arriving at his apartment unexpectedly.

"That's okay, although you caught me at a bad time. I was just about to leave for work. Is everything alright as it is unlike you to drop in without prior notice?"

Rohit asked Gurudev.

"Well, as a matter of fact, I am here to find out about Meeta," Gurudev answered.

"Meeta went to see her mother yesterday, and I haven't heard from her since," Rohit said.

"I am concerned about Meeta as we were to meet for dinner yesterday, but she never showed up at the venue and neither did she call to tell me that it's cancelled. And when I tried to contact her on her cell phone it came switched off, while her landline went to the answering machine. As I was worried about her, I dropped by Meeta's apartment this morning to enquire about her well-being, but I found the place locked. And she does not appear to have returned home either," Gurudev said.

"And how can I be of any help?" Rohit queried.

"I thought perhaps Meeta would have kept you informed about her whereabouts. Do you know where she is? And do you have any idea where she could be?"

Gurudev asked Rohit.

"I am afraid I don't know where Meeta is. And should she get in touch with me, I'll ask her to give you a call."

Rohit denied having any knowledge of Meeta's whereabouts. And in spite of being well aware that she was no more, and that Gurudev would never see her or hear from her again, Rohit did not give the latter any indication that his ex-wife was dead. And Gurudev had no inkling that Meeta had passed away. Should he suspect the authenticity of the automobile crash which had claimed his ex-wife's life, he would leave no stone unturned to unearth the truth behind the fatal accident. And it would not be long before he stumbled upon the truth and discovered that Rohit was instrumental for her death. And since Rohit did not want Gurudev to learn the truth about Meeta's death, he chose to feign ignorance.

#

Raveena was not her usual self at work this morning as she looked rather grim. And she did not greet Rohit with the customary "good morning" when he entered the office.

"Is everything alright with you?" Rohit asked his secretary. "It's unlike you to be so glum," he remarked.

"Yes, all is well," Raveena replied.

"Are you sure? Or would you rather take the day off and go home?" Rohit asked. He wondered whether Raveena was having trouble with her boyfriend again. It was no secret that she was in a bad relationship, and he was well aware of his secretary's troubled love life. However, he would never have guessed that Meeta was the cause of Raveena's gloom, and that she was the reason his secretary was grieving.

Meeta was Raveena's cousin by virtue of their mothers being siblings, and the latter was devastated by her death. Meeta's passing was an irreparable loss, and Raveena would never be able to get over losing her beloved cousin.

Raveena had accidently chanced upon the racy photos of Rohit and Rahul together when she had gone to place some papers in the safe. And she had tried to blackmail Rohit by mailing copies of the snapshots to his residence before placing a series of phone calls to him. In fact, she had worked out a perfect plan for extortion without her coming into the picture until she caught Rohit regarding her with suspicion.

And when she realized that Rohit suspected her of being the blackmailer, Raveena developed cold feet, and she returned the photographs, but not before she had retained copies of the snapshots with her. When Rohit expressed his desire to end his casual sexual relationship with Meeta, Raveena coerced her cousin to blackmail him with the pictures in exchange for an astronomical sum. Raveena now regretted having goaded her cousin to resort to extortion as had it not been for her, Meeta would still be alive. And she blamed herself for her cousin's passing.

Raveena was pretty certain that Rohit was behind Meeta's death and that the automobile crash which had killed her cousin was not just a mere accident, but an orchestrated collision to have her eliminated. And she was quite sure that Meeta's death was a cold-blooded murder that was committed at Rohit's behest. However, despite being aware that Rohit was instrumental for Meeta's death, Raveena felt helpless since she could not nail the fatal road accident to him nor could she prove his hand in her cousin's passing.

CHAPTER 27

Gia had just emerged from the shower when she felt a sudden bout of giddiness, and she attributed the dizzy nauseous spell to the mushrooms which she had eaten the night before. As she appeared to have been quite fine the previous night, she could not think of anything else besides the mushrooms that could have made her sick. And she sought to get some relief by having lemonade with ice.

She had acquired a taste for sour, tangy foods of late, and she found herself indulging in a lot of sauces and pickles lately. And the sight and smell of certain foods seemed to nauseate her, and it appeared to make her quite sick. She was taken completely by surprise when she vomited while at work later that day as the hamburger which she had at the fast food joint for lunch appeared to have been stale. And she could not help throwing up the meal which she had eaten a short while ago.

Gia turned to conventional home remedies to rid her of the biliousness but it was of no avail, as there was no respite from the nausea. And when she resorted to over the counter medication, it only provided her with temporary relief; as the nausea was soon back once the effect of the pill had worn off.

"I don't know what's wrong with me these days since I am nauseous all the time." Gia voiced her concern about her delicate health to her friend, Mandira.

"You must have gotten some sort of an ailment, and perhaps you are ill," Mandira stated.

"I don't know. Anyways, what do you suggest I do?"

Gia asked Mandira.

"I think you should see a doctor for the right diagnosis, and he should be able to get to the root of your problem," Mandira replied.

"Do you really think that I should show myself to the doctor? Is that really necessary?" Gia asked.

"Yes, definitely," Mandira reiterated, "in fact, I can fix an appointment with Dr. Burman for you if you like.

"Well, in that case, I would like you to fix an appointment with Dr. Burman for me," Gia affirmed. "And try to get the earliest appointment."

#

Dr. Palat Burman was a well known General Practitioner who had his private practice at Chowpatty. Dr. Burman examined Gia thoroughly before arriving at his diagnosis.

"So far as I can see, there does not appear to be anything wrong with you. And you are fine," Dr. Burman stated.

"Are you saying that this visit was unnecessary?"Gia asked.

"Well, not entirely."

"What do you mean?"

"I would recommend that you consult a gynaecologist to seek a second opinion. Perhaps, the gynac would be able to arrive at the right diagnosis," Dr. Burman said.

"That's quite ridiculous as I am not pregnant. And a visit to the gynac is not necessary," Gia averred.

"You may be right, but then your symptoms are reminiscent of a pregnancy. And it would be better to have a gynaecologist examine you," Dr. Burman reiterated.

"It's impossible that I could be pregnant, and it is probably a misdiagnosis." Gia dismissed Dr. Burman's diagnosis of a possible pregnancy as nothing but mere speculation since it was well-nigh impossible for her to have conceived. She had not been in a serious relationship since her fiancé had passed away, and so far as Amar and she were concerned, theirs was a platonic relationship. And even the thought of bedding her best friend was sacrilegious.

There was, however, no let-up or relief from the nausea which only seemed to get worse with each passing day, and Gia found herself throwing up practically every morning. And when she collapsed in the bathroom one morning while vomiting, she decided that it was time to heed Dr. Burman's advice.

#

Dr. Leela Warrior was a reputed obstetrician and gynaecologist who was attached to the prestigious Hinduja

Hospital and her list of clients included some of the well known names of the city. She had treated Gia for a vaginal infection sometime ago, and the latter was now a regular patient of hers. Dr. Warrior first examined Gia before asking her to get an ultrasound done. Then, Gia heard the last thing that she expected to hear.

"You are pregnant," Dr. Warrior stated, after the ultrasound.

The news of her pregnancy came as a terrible shock to Gia as it was impossible for her to have conceived. Besides, apart from the nausea, she had not displayed any of the obvious signs of a pregnancy; for example; a bloated belly. Moreover, she had a regular menstrual cycle and her weight had remained constant too.

"Are you quite certain that I am pregnant? And that you've not made a mistake?"

Gia asked Dr. Warrior.

"Yes, I'm positive you are pregnant and there is no mistake with the diagnosis. As a matter of fact, you are now into the second trimester, and you are almost five months pregnant," Dr. Warrior reiterated.

"How can that be when I'm having a regular period?"

Gia asked Dr Warrior.

"Yours is a type of "no signs" pregnancy that happens in very rare instances. Blood vessels in the lower part of the uterus may have been bleeding, which explains the regular period. And since the bleeding did not affect the fetus, the baby continued to grow." Dr. Warrior explained Gia's pregnancy despite the absence of the usual changes.

Gia could not quite understand how she could have conceived when she had not been with anyone recently, and she was puzzled as to how the pregnancy could have occurred. And even as she tried to gather her wits together and searched for an answer to her current predicament, she had a sudden flash, and she realized what had led to her present condition.

She had been to a party with her friend, Brij, sometime ago where alcohol had flowed as freely as water, and pretty soon all the guests were drunk. Before long; they shed their inhibitions, and they gradually began to disrobe as the hours passed by until they were as naked as the day they were born. And they soon sought to indulge in carnal activities with perfect strangers. Gia could not recall who she was with at the time, and she was not even certain whether she was with Brij or whether she had switched partners. She was far too drunk at the party to remember anything since the alcohol had dimmed her senses, and she had participated in the goings-on without any reservation. Her only concern at that moment was the erotic pleasure which she had been starved of for so long, and she had indulged her carnal craving. Everything was such a blur at the time that she was pretty certain she had imagined the whole incident. The truth, however, was staring her in the face now, and she realized that the said event was not just a mere figment of her imagination, but that it had actually occurred. And that she was paying far too great a price for her drunken folly.

"What do I do now? I don't want this baby," Gia said.

"I am sorry, but I would not advise an abortion at this stage as it's rather risky, and you could end up losing your life," Dr. Warrior replied.

#

Gia was dismayed to know that she had no other option but to carry the baby to term and that she had no other choice but to give birth to the child. And since she did not want to be burdened by an unwanted pregnancy and be saddled with a bastard, she would have to think of an immediate solution in order to avoid such an awful scenario.

She had an undated prescription for Valium that was meant for her mother and which was never used. And she sought to put the doctor's prescription to good use now. She wrote out the current date on the prescription before proceeding to the drug store, and she waited until the store was pretty crowded before approaching the pharmacist.

"I need these sedatives for my mother," Gia stated, whilst handing the prescription to the pharmacist.

The overworked pharmacist was far too busy attending to his numerous customers to notice the different shades of ink that appeared on the doctor's prescription. And he gave the sedatives to Gia without raising a fuss.

Once Gia returned home with the tranquilizers, she had a difficult time trying to convince herself to take the next step. And she struggled with her conscience briefly before resorting to execute her morbid plan. Gia swallowed a handful of the Valium in combination with a bottle of vodka. The deadly cocktail of tranquilizers and alcohol would shortly take effect, and her misery would end soon.

She, however, panicked immediately after her suicidal bid when she realized that she had made a grave mistake. And she acknowledged that hers was an act of sheer desperation that was committed on the spur of the moment. Gia regretted her decision to end her life in the very next instant since she did not wish to die.

As the Valium was gradually starting to take effect, Gia was beginning to feel drowsy, and she was slowly losing her bearings. And it would not be long before she fell asleep never to awaken from her drug induced slumber. Time was running out for her, and she would soon be dead. And she required medical attention post-haste as any delay on her part would result in her death. Gia picked up the phone from the table, and she called the suicide help line, and even as she dialed the telephone number, her fingers trembled. And it was an effort for her to make the phone call.

The operator at the suicide help line responded promptly to the call, and she answered Gia right away.

"This is the suicide help line. And how may I be of help?"

The operator asked Gia.

"I am afraid I have taken too many sleeping pills by mistake, and I am going to die. I need help immediately," Gia said.

"Can I have an address?" The operator asked.

"No 6 Sea heights, A Road, Churchgate, Behind Jai Hind College. And could you please hurry?" Gia beseeched. She was beginning to slur and her eyes were sleep laden, and she feared that she would be dead when help arrived.

The ambulance arrived shortly after Gia had placed the call to the suicide help line service. And the paramedics lost no time in reaching her apartment. Gia had almost passed out by the time the paramedics got to her place, and she was barely conscious when they lifted her on to the stretcher and carried her to the ambulance.

Gia was rushed to the nearest hospital, and she was administered immediate medical attention. She was taken to the Emergency Room where her stomach was pumped out and the deadly cocktail was flushed from her system. She had managed to beat death by a mere whisker, and she was fortunate to be alive. Gia would be required to remain in the hospital for the next couple of days before she was allowed to return home.

#

Jhanvi was shocked to learn that Gia had attempted suicide, and she could not understand what had driven her daughter to kill herself. As her daughter was not the sort who would want to take her own life, Jhanvi was pretty certain that something was amiss for Gia to have taken such a drastic step. And she was determined to get to the bottom of her daughter's suicide bid. She resolved to unravel the mystery behind Gia's desperation to take her own life.

Jhanvi turned to her rakhi brother, Akash Jha, for help, and she expressed her concern about Gia to him. Though Jhanvi and Akash were not kin they, however, shared the bond of siblings, and Akash was very protective of Jhanvi's daughter, Gia.

"I'm really very worried about Gia, and I fail to understand why she tried to kill herself. And why on earth would she want to commit suicide?"

Jhanvi said to Akash.

"I am sure Gia will be fine. Sometimes youngsters tend to do foolish things on impulse without giving a thought to the consequences. And they tend to regret what they've done later," Akash replied.

"I am not so sure that Gia's suicide bid was an impulsive act. And I'm quite certain there is a very good reason behind her attempted suicide," Jhanvi stated.

"And what makes you so sure that there is more to Gia's suicide bid than meets the eye? And why are you so certain that something is amiss?"

Akash asked Jhanvi.

"That's because Gia clammed up when I tried to probe the reason why she attempted to kill herself. And that is unlike her as she has always been very honest with me," she answered.

"Give her time and I am sure she will open up to you. It's too soon. And besides, I think you are reading too much into what happened," Akash stated.

"I somehow cannot help getting the impression that all is not well with Gia. And that she is hiding something from me. You may call it a mother's instinct if you like," Jhanvi reiterated.

"I want you to stop worrying about Gia and I assure you that I'll take care of everything. Trust me. I will confront Gia and get the truth out of her. Leave it to me to deal with your daughter," Akash said.

"Alright, I'm relying on you to find out why my daughter tried to kill herself," Jhanvi replied.

"And you can rest assured that I will get to the bottom of it, and ferret the truth out of Gia if I have to," Akash declared.

#

Akash visited Gia at the hospital later that day.

"Your mother is worried sick about you. She wants me to find out why you tried to kill yourself. Why did you attempt suicide?"

Akash asked Gia.

"I guess I was being foolish at the time," Gia replied.

"I don't buy that explanation as people don't try to end their lives because they are foolish. I am sure there is a good reason behind your attempted suicide, and I want you to be honest with me. And don't try to lie because I won't give up until I hear the truth from you," Akash averred.

"I am pregnant," Gia said.

"What do you mean that you are pregnant? And are you really serious?"

Akash asked Gia.

"Yes, I am afraid so," Gia affirmed.

"You are a real disgrace, and I am ashamed of you," Akash said.

"I'm sorry you feel that way," Gia replied.

"You are damn right I do. And who is the man who got you pregnant and then disappeared?"

Akash asked Gia.

Akash Jha was an erstwhile member of the dreaded khap, and with him family honor came first. He had not spared his own daughter in his bid to protect the family name. When she eloped with a boy of lower social strata, he had the couple hunted and gunned down, and their death was spoken of in hushed whispers as none had the courage to confront him with the truth.

Akash would never forgive Gia if he were to learn that she did not know who the father of her child was, and he would brand her a slut and a woman of loose morals. He loathed women of such ilk as they brought shame to the family, and he felt that they did not deserve to live. He would not hesitate to have Gia eliminated in order to protect the family name, and she would become the victim of an honor killing.

Since Gia did not want to fall prey to an honor killing and meet the same fate as Akash's daughter, her only thought at the moment was to save her own skin. "Amar…" she said, mentioning the first name that came to her mind. "Amar is the father of my child."

"Are you trying to tell me that it was Amar who got you pregnant?"

Akash asked Gia.

"Yes," Gia reiterated; lying brazenly. She was terrified of the consequences of her drunken folly, and her sole concern at the moment was to ensure that she did not end up dead. And even if it meant that it was at Amar's expense.

"Well, I will be damned. The young man shall certainly pay for this," Akash thundered.

CHAPTER 28

A messenger dropped by at Stan Express Bank late in the afternoon to deliver a handwritten note to Amar. The short, crisp note was sent to him by Akash Jha, and it contained a brief message.

"I would like to see you urgently, and I am sorry for this short notice. Meet me after work today, and I won't take no for an answer. I will be waiting for you at New Yorkers around 7.30 P. M. this evening. Akash." The message read.

"I need an answer," the messenger stated. "I've been told not to return without a reply."

"Tell Akash that I will be there," Amar affirmed, before dismissing the messenger.

#

Amar got ready to leave for his appointment with Akash Jha after completing his work for the day. However, even before he could step out of the office, he was detained by Rohit. "I know that you were getting ready to leave, and I am sorry to keep you back at the last minute. But as this is rather urgent, it can't wait until tomorrow morning, and I'd like you to attend to this immediately." He handed Amar a file.

#

Amar tried to reach New Yorkers as quickly as he could, and when he arrived at the venue, he found Akash Jha waiting for him. And he appeared to be pretty annoyed.

"I thought you had stood me up, and was about to leave the place." Akash voiced his displeasure at having been kept waiting.

"I am sorry for the delay as I got held up at work. And that was quite unexpected," Amar replied.

Since Amar had left immediately after work he was rather hungry and he wanted to eat. And he was tempted to ask for a pizza. However, Akash's demeanor deterred him from placing an order.

Akash Jha looked grim and a disapproving frown puckered his brow, and it was quite evident that this was not a courtesy meeting. Amar was pretty certain that they were not assembled here to discuss their health or the weather, but that this meeting had a far serious connotation.

"Have you heard from Gia lately?"

Akash asked Amar.

"As a matter of fact, I have not heard from Gia in a while, and that is quite unlike her as she calls me every day," Amar said. "Is everything alright with her?"

"I am afraid all is not well with Gia since she is in the hospital for attempting to take her own life," Akash replied.

"Are you serious? And why on earth would Gia try to kill herself?"

Amar asked Akash.

"You mean to say you don't know why Gia attempted suicide?" Akash queried.

"No, I have absolutely no idea why Gia made a bid at her life. In fact; this is news to me," Amar averred.

"It is all because of you that Gia tried to end her life, and you are the reason she tried to kill herself. And you are instrumental for her trying to attempt suicide," Akash said.

"And what do you mean by saying that I am the reason Gia tried to kill herself? I fail to understand why I am being blamed for her attempted suicide," Amar said.

"That's because you got her pregnant and left her in the lurch thereafter. And she panicked since she does not want to have a child out of wedlock," Akash reiterated.

"That's utter nonsense. And it's really absurd that I'm being blamed for her condition as I had absolutely no idea that Gia was pregnant," Amar averred.

"Are you trying to tell me that you are not responsible for getting Gia pregnant? Am I to assume that Gia's pregnancy is the result of an immaculate conception?" Akash queried sardonically.

"All I am saying is that I am not responsible for Gia's pregnancy. Gia and I are good friends, and we share a platonic relationship, and nothing beyond that. And I'm offended by the aspersion that is being cast upon me."

"Are you saying that you did not sleep with Gia? And that the two of you never ended up in bed together?"

Akash asked Amar.

"Yes, and that's precisely what I mean," Amar affirmed. "Not only did I never sleep with Gia; I could never ever dream of sleeping with her as it would be blasphemous to bed my best friend."

"Stop lying to me since Gia told me that it was you who got her pregnant. And I was feigning ignorance in spite of knowing the truth, as I had hoped that you would be honest with me," Akash said.

"That's nothing but a lie since I never touched Gia, I swear."

Amar denied the accusation that was being leveled against him. He was completely in the dark about Gia's pregnancy, and being accused of getting her pregnant was like adding insult to injury.

"That's what all men say when they get caught. They want to have their fun, but they don't want to take responsibility for what they have done," Akash thundered.

"But, that's the absolute truth," Amar reiterated.

"I've heard enough of your lies and I won't stand for anymore of it. And I will give you an ultimatum. If you know what's good for you, you'll own up to the truth or else you will be real sorry," Akash averred.

"The truth is that I never got Gia pregnant, and the baby is not mine." Amar attempted to establish his innocence, but he sounded unconvincing even to himself. He was beginning to feel helpless and he realized that he was wasting his breath trying to convince Akash that he was not responsible for Gia's pregnancy. And that he could cry himself hoarse declaring he was innocent, but it would all be in vain since Akash would never believe him. Akash Jha was pretty certain that Amar was instrumental for Gia's pregnancy, and he believed that the latter was the father of her child. And that nothing that Amar said in his defense would convince Akash Jha of otherwise.

"Don't you put on that innocent act with me since I know your kind? You get women pregnant, and then refuse to own up to it. Now, if you value your life, you will do as I say, and you will marry Gia at the earliest," Akash said. He rose to leave after issuing that threat, and he stormed out of the pizza joint. And Amar was left staring helplessly after him.

CHAPTER 29

Amar was at Sea Heights to see Gia who had prior intimation of his arrival. He greeted the doorman at the entrance before stepping into the building and proceeding to the elevator to reach the 15th floor. Gia resided all by herself in a one bedroom rented apartment, and the tiny flat was sparsely furnished with the bare minimum furniture to the extent that even the television set was portable.

Since he did not want to inconvenience Gia by have her answer the door, Amar let himself into her apartment with the spare key that was kept in his custody. Gia, however, was not present at home, and she appeared to be out. Amar decided to wait at the apartment until Gia showed up, and he made himself comfortable in her absence. He helped himself to beer from the refrigerator before settling down on the couch to watch soccer on the portable television. Though the telecast was a re-run of last week's match, he decided to watch the game all the same as he had missed catching the match live. Amar had barely tuned in to the sports channel and adjusted the volume on the television set, when he heard the sound of the door open. He turned around to greet Gia, but was surprised to find a mean looking man framed at the doorway instead.

"You seem to have come to the wrong apartment." Amar stated, even as he wondered how the stranger's key managed to open the door.

"Is this where Gia Kapoor lives?"

The stranger asked Amar.

"Yes, this is her apartment, alright," Amar affirmed.

"Then, I am at the right place as that's where I'm supposed to be," the stranger declared.

"Well, I am afraid Gia is not at home. And, you will have to come by later if you wish to meet her," Amar said.

"I haven't come here for Gia. As a matter of fact, I have been told to fetch you," the stranger answered.

"This is a real surprise since I had no idea that I was wanted. And who may I ask has sent you for me?"

Amar asked the stranger.

"I have been sent by my boss to take you to him," the stranger answered.

"And who is your boss?" Amar queried."Does he have a name?"

"I'm sorry, but I am not at liberty to disclose that information." The stranger declined to enlighten Amar.

"I'm afraid there's been some kind of a mix up, and I am probably not the person you are seeking. This must be a case of mistaken identity," Amar said.

"No, this isn't the case of a mistaken identity, and I know what I am doing. I have been specifically instructed to fetch you, and you'll do as you are told or else you will end up dead. Now, I want you to come with me without making any fuss. And if you so much as even try to raise an alarm, you will have your brains blown out," the stranger hissed, before holding a gun to Amar's head.

Amar had no clue of what was happening, and he did not have the faintest idea of what was going on. And he could not hazard a guess as to what the mean looking man was up to. However, with a loaded gun pointed to his head, he had little choice but to do as he was told, and to follow the stranger's instructions. He was quite certain that the gunman would not hesitate to carry out his threat if he failed to heed his command or tried to offer any resistance. The armed stranger made his intentions pretty clear, and Amar did not wish to put him to the test. He left Gia's apartment without any fuss or ado, and he meekly followed the gunman's instructions without attempting to put up a fight.

The gunman followed closely behind Amar, and his finger never left the trigger of the firearm. He led Amar to a car which was waiting for them at the kerb.

"Get inside the car."

The armed stranger ordered Amar to enter the vehicle before following suit. And he sat down next to Amar in the rear seat, with the gun held against the latter's head. They drove around the city for a while before the car finally came to a grinding halt in front of a small hall.

"Get inside the hall without trying to draw any attention to yourself. And if you should even so much as attempt to squeak, you'll be real sorry," the gunman warned Amar.

Amar alighted from the vehicle, and he proceeded to the hall. And when he stepped inside, he saw Akash who was accompanied by a pundit.

"Why am I not surprised to see you here? I should have known that you were instrumental for my abduction. What the hell is this place anyway and why am I here?"

Amar asked Akash.

"What do you think is going on here? Why don't you take a wild guess?" Akash mocked Amar.

"How the hell would I know what's going on here? You tell me since you are the mastermind behind the whole plot," Amar answered.

"Well, if you must know; there is going to be a wedding. And, yours, to be very specific; you see you'll be getting married shortly," Akash stated.

"Is this some kind of a joke?"

Amar asked Akash.

"I'm afraid not," Akash replied. "I am dead serious."

"Have you gone completely mad? What in God's name are you talking about?"

Amar asked Akash.

"Why is it so difficult for you to understand that Gia and you are getting married today? This is an Arya Samaj Hall, and the pundit will conduct your wedding according to the rituals," Akash reiterated.

"That is utter nonsense. And I don't believe a word of what you are saying," Amar said.

"Well, you will know shortly whether it's nonsense or not. And you can see for yourself whether I am lying or telling you the truth," Akash answered.

"I need to see Gia right away, and I demand an immediate audience with her." Amar said. "Where the hell is she?" He asked Akash.

"Have some patience as she will be with you shortly. The bride is getting ready since she wants to look her best on her big day," Akash replied.

"Don't you try to patronize me? I am sure Gia would never agree to take part in this sham wedding, or for that matter be willing to go through with this ridiculous charade," Amar stated.

"Then I am afraid, that's where you are wrong. This was all Gia's idea after all," Akash retorted.

"I don't believe you for a moment as I am pretty certain that it's nothing but complete bullshit. I know Gia well enough, and she would never be up to anything of this sort. I'm sure you're lying," Amar said.

"Well, Gia is here. Why don't you ask her yourself? Perhaps, you will get your answer then," Akash replied.

Amar turned around to see Gia enter the hall. She was dressed in a wedding gear, and she was in bridal attire as she was draped in a bright red silk sari with jewelry to match. And she looked every inch the blushing bride.

"Akash tells me that this is all your idea? Is it true? And tell me he is wrong, and that you won't agree to go through with this charade."

Amar addressed Gia.

"I'm really very sorry Amar, but I had no other choice." Gia replied.

CHAPTER 30

The wedding was being held behind closed doors, and the hall was shut to the general public at large. There were about half a dozen people in attendance at the venue which included Akash and his two associates, apart from the bride and the groom. The sixth person present on the occasion was the pundit who would be presiding over the ceremony, and he would conduct the nuptials according to the Arya Samaj rites. Though it was not the kind of wedding which Gia had always dreamed about, it was, however, the best that could be done given the unusual circumstances.

The gunman stood guard over Amar, and he had his eyes trained on his captive. And he never let the latter out of his sight even for a split second. The gunman's gaze was glued firmly on Amar since he never let his eyes wander, and he was like a hawk that was keeping a keen watch over its prey. And he would not hesitate to swoop for the kill the instant that Amar made a suspicious move.

Amar was desperate to get away from the place, and he wanted to flee from the clutches of his captors. However, with a loaded gun pointed at his head, he had little choice but to remain captive, and to heed his captors' bidding. He could either take a bullet by refusing to marry Gia, or he could surrender to the situation and agree to go through with the wedding. And Amar figured that it was far better to go through with the motions of the sham wedding and marry Gia rather than to end up dead, as the marriage could always be annulled at a later date whereas he could never be resurrected from the dead and be brought back to life. And given the bizarre circumstances, Amar felt that it was prudent to be practical and play along with the situation rather than to be foolish and risk losing his life.

The pundit was specifically instructed to keep the ritual as brief as possible, and he was told to ensure that the ceremony was not lengthy and long drawn out. It would have to be the shortest wedding that he had ever performed, and the nuptials would have to end almost as soon as it had begun.

"Try to keep the ceremony as short as possible. It should be brief and simple without going into too much detail since time is a constraint here."

Akash said to the pundit.

"And it shall be a very brief ceremony," the pundit replied.

"I remembered to bring along the required items necessary to conduct a proper wedding. I have here the floral garlands for the bridal couple to exchange, as well as the vermillion and the mangalsutra without which the wedding would not be complete." Akash stated, handing the relevant articles to the pundit. And he ensured that the wedding would be conducted in accordance with tradition.

The pundit lit the sacred fire before summoning the couple to the mandap or the altar. "I am all set to commence the ceremony. And I'd like the bridal couple to take their seat at the mandap," he announced.

Amar had to literally drag his feet to the altar, and it was a herculean effort for him to take every step that brought him closer to his doom. He knew that he was cornered and that he could not escape his impending fate, and that nothing short of a miracle would stop the wedding now. And although Amar did not quite believe in miracles, he fervently prayed for one such occurrence at this instant as he desperately invoked his God.

Gia would be given away in marriage to Amar by Akash who would perform the kanyadhan or the gifting of the bride to the groom. And he would play the role of father of the bride. Ideally, Gia would have liked to have her father give her away in marriage, and Gul too looked forward to the day when he would see his daughter a bride. However, given the circumstances, her father was not present at the wedding as her parents were unaware that she was getting married today. And they had no inkling that it was their daughter's wedding day.

The bridal couple exchanged the garlands or the varamala before taking their seat at the mandap. And once they were seated, the priest began to conduct the wedding by chanting the holy mantras before asking the couple to commence the seven rounds around the holy fire.

Amar took the lead, and he led Gia around the havan or the holy fire. And they had barely taken three rounds around the sacred fire when they were rudely interrupted by the sound of the door being flung open, and they realized that they had an intruder amongst their midst.

They were surprised to see Jhanvi enter the hall, and she was the last person who they had expected to show up at the venue of the wedding.

"How the hell did you manage to get here? And how did you even know that we were here in the first place?"

Akash asked Jhanvi.

"That's not really relevant here. Firstly, tell me how could you collude with Gia and offer your assistance to carry out her devious plan. I expected you to be more sensible, and be wise enough not to go along with her crazy idea? And I thought you had more sense not to be a party to Gia's shenanigans," Jhanvi said to Akash.

"It was all Gia's idea, I swear. And I had nothing whatsoever to do with it. In fact, I tried my best to dissuade your daughter from going through with this charade, but she was not willing to listen to me," Akash replied.

"Well then, you should have known better than to side with my daughter. And you should've refused to play a part in Amar's abduction, and you should've declined to hold him captive," Jhanvi stated.

"I tried to talk Gia out of the whole thing by telling her what she was doing was wrong, but she would not heed me. And when she pleaded with me for my help, I could not bring myself to refuse. You know how I am when it comes to Gia, and I'm sorry that I let my emotions get the better of me," Akash said.

Gia could barely contain her shock at seeing Jhanvi, and she could not quite believe that her mother was here. She wondered how her mother had found out about the wedding when no one knew that she was getting married today. As the wedding was top secret, she had not breathed a word about it to anyone, and no one had any inkling that today was her wedding day.

"Mamma, what are you doing here?"

Gia asked Jhanvi.

"Did you really think that I would not find out about the wedding? Things have a way of getting out, you know," Jhanvi answered.

"Seriously mamma, I told no one about today. And nobody has any idea that I'm getting married in this particular hall," Gia reiterated.

"Well, that's what you think, but your friend, Mandira, knew all about the wedding and that includes the venue as well. And she could not quite stop herself from telling me. Mandira is instrumental for leaking out your wedding plans," Jhanvi said.

"How did Mandira manage to find out about the wedding anyways since I didn't tell her either? And how on earth did she know that I was getting married today?"

Gia asked Jhanvi.

Mandira was Gia's best friend and confidante, and she never hid anything from her. She usually took Mandira into confidence, and she told her friend about everything that was going on in her life. Gia, however, chose to remain mum in this particular instance since she could not risk a spoiler to her plans by letting anyone know that she was getting married today; lest someone should try to stop the wedding. And as there was far too much at stake; Gia had chosen to keep Mandira in the dark about today.

"I know you didn't mention anything about the wedding to Mandira and she was hurt since you did not take her into confidence. And she felt offended that you did not trust her enough to keep your secret. After all, Mandira is your best friend, and she expected you to confide in her," Jhanvi averred.

"Then how did Mandira find out about the wedding? And did she tell you out of spite, just to get me into trouble?" Gia asked. She was curious to know how Mandira had come to learn about the wedding when no one apart from Akash and her knew that she was getting married today. And as neither of them had mentioned about the wedding to anyone, it was a mystery as to how her friend had managed to get wind of the nuptials.

"Well; Mandira overheard your conversation with uncle Akash. Rather, I should say that she eavesdropped on the two of you while you were discussing your clandestine wedding. She was at the table next to yours at the Starbucks coffee shop, and as the two or you were rather engrossed in your discussion, you failed to notice her presence at the café.

And that's how she was privy to your wedding plans," Jhanvi elucidated; furnishing the answer to her daughter's query.

"Mandira should have come to me first before going behind my back," Gia stated.

"Apparently, she did try to get the truth out of you, but you chose to lie to her instead," Jhanvi replied.

"I do remember her asking me about the wedding, and I brushed off the topic at the time. And I told her that it wasn't true," Gia said.

Mandira had confronted Gia shortly after her meeting with Akash and she asked the latter whether she was getting married, but Gia had denied the truth at the time. Although she had felt terribly guilty for lying to her best friend, she, however, felt that it was in her own interest to hide the truth from Mandira.

"Well, Mandira asked you for the truth but you chose to lie to her instead," Jhanvi reiterated.

"Whatever it may be, it's certainly not Mandira's business to inform you," Gia said. She was annoyed with Mandira for telling on her as her friend had no right to interfere in her life. And she decided to put an end to their friendship that very instant. Gia swore that she would no longer be friends with Mandira, and she vowed never to speak to the latter again.

"Well, if it makes you happy; I didn't quite believe Mandira when she told me that you were getting married in this hall today. And even though I was pretty certain that she was trying to pull my leg, I came here all the same to ensure that she was not lying." Jhanvi explained her presence in the hall.

"I'm sorry that I didn't think it fit to keep you informed about today as I feared that you would disapprove of my modus operandi. However, once I've explained myself you will understand that I was compelled by circumstances to resort to Amar's abduction, and that I was left with no other option," Gia stated.

"No, don't even try to find an excuse for what you are doing. And neither do I want to know the reason why you chose to do what you did. All I want is for you to put an end to this sham right now before it's too late. Stop this madness immediately, and forget about going through with the nuptials."

"Mamma, please don't make such a big deal out of it. It's only a wedding for God's sakes. And it happens all the time," Gia said. She could not understand why her mother was upset with her over such a trivial issue. After all, she was only getting married, and she was not about to commit a heinous crime such as murder.

"I know it's only a wedding but it's a sham wedding since Amar is being forced to marry you at gun point. And that is not right," Jhanvi declared.

"Mamma, you certainly can't afford to preach to me."

Gia taunted her mother.

"And what do you mean by that? Just what are you trying to insinuate?" Jhanvi demanded to know what her daughter meant by her heavily loaded statement.

"Do you really want me to spell it out for you?"

Gia asked Jhanvi.

"Yes, please do. I'd like to hear what you have to say."

"I know that daddy is not my father. And that uncle Akash's brother is my parent," Gia replied.

"That's utter rubbish," Jhanvi exclaimed.

"Stop denying it mamma as I have known the truth for a long time. Nani told me so herself. She said that you were to marry uncle Akash's brother who then decided to seek nirvana in the Himalayas instead, and that you were pregnant at the time he went away to the mountains. As uncle Akash was a married man, he persuaded his best friend to marry you to save your reputation. And that's how daddy became my father when I am actually uncle Akash's niece," Gia reiterated.

Jhanvi and Madhav were childhood sweethearts, and it was understood that they would marry someday. However, Madhav's short stint at an ashram led to him turning spiritual, and he decided to renounce the material world in search of nirvana. He retired to the mountains to spend his days among nature in meditation and prayer. With Jhanvi pregnant at the time; she turned to Madhav's brother, Akash, to bail her out, before he convinced his friend to come to her rescue and to be her knight in shining armour by marrying her to legitimize the child.

"But that doesn't absolve you of what you are doing," Jhanvi stated.

"Maybe, but then you are no saint either, so you can't afford to deliver a sermon." Gia continued to taunt her mother.

"I know that I am not perfect, but what you're doing is absolutely wrong," Jhanvi averred.

"Don't try to tell me what's right and what's wrong since it sounds slanderous coming from someone like you," Gia retorted.

"Are you trying to tell me that you are hell-bent upon going ahead with this wedding?"

Jhanvi asked her daughter.

"Yes, you are damn right mamma. I'm certainly going ahead with the nuptials," Gia declared.

"And, nothing that I say is going to stop you from what you are about to do?"

"I am afraid so," Gia affirmed.

"Well, I can't stand by and allow you to destroy Amar's life after I assured him that nothing of this sort would ever happen. You see, I gave Amar my word that I would do everything in my power to protect his interest."

"And, when exactly was that?" Gia asked Jhanvi. "This is news to me since I had no idea that Amar had sought your help."

"Amar came to see me shortly after his meeting with Akash. And he was upset as the latter had threatened him with dire consequences should he refuse to marry you.

I assured him at the time that he had nothing to fear as something of that sort would never happen. And I told Amar that under no circumstances would you agree to marry him - not even at Akash's behest. However, I can now see that I was wrong since I obviously didn't know my daughter well enough to speak on her behalf. And I'm really disappointed that I let Amar down."

"I'm sorry, mamma, but I am not going to change my mind. And you're wasting your time trying to convince me to listen to you," Gia said. She was annoyed with Jhanvi for taking Amar's side as she had expected her mother to understand her plight. She was only trying to secure her child's future by giving it a father's name. And marriage was a necessary part of that plan.

"Then, I am afraid you leave me with no other choice," Jhanvi stated, before turning towards the gunman and grabbing the pistol from him. She snatched the gun from right out of his hand and pointed the firearm towards Gia before taking careful aim and firing a shot at her daughter.

Gia, however, had the presence of mind to duck in the nick of time to dodge the bullet which missed her by a hair's breadth as it flew past her to get embedded in the door. Even as Jhanvi cocked the gun and took aim to fire a second shot at her daughter; Akash wrested the firearm from her. The gun, however, went off in the ensuing struggle and a shot was fired. And the discharged bullet hit the wall before ricocheting off it and getting lodged in Jhanvi's spine.

CHAPTER 31

Amar fled from the hall in the chaos that followed the shooting as his captors were left badly shaken by the unexpected turn of events to pay any heed to him. As all their attention was now focused on the injured Jhanvi who lay bleeding on the floor; they were far too busy tending to her, to spare a thought to their captive. And Amar took advantage of the situation to flee from the place, and he availed of the opportunity to slip away unnoticed. He left the hall as quickly as he could, and he got away from his captors post-haste since he wanted to be completely out of sight when his abductors realized that he was missing.

Once he had exited from the hall, Amar searched for a taxi to take him home before hailing the first cab that he saw. And he was cautious whilst boarding the vehicle since he took every precaution to ensure that no one was coming after him. Amar glanced furtively over his shoulder to ascertain that he was not followed, and that no one was chasing after him. He was relieved to see that he had succeeded in fleeing from the place unnoticed, and that he had managed to get away from the hall without drawing any attention to himself.

The taxi driver was told to leave immediately since Amar did not wish to take a chance by lingering around any longer than was necessary. And he did not want to waste any more time remaining in the vicinity of his abductors lest he should be discovered. Amar was afraid that his presence would be missed at any time, and he feared that his captors would come looking for him once they realized that he was gone. And he desired to be as far away as possible when his absence finally dawned upon his captors. Amar did not want to be taken hostage for a second time, and he did not wish to be held captive again.

"I want you to go as fast as the legal limit permits you. And you've to race past all the amber lights before the signals turn red as I don't wish to slow down or stop anywhere until I reach my destination."

Amar instructed the taxi driver.

"Yes, of course, and you can rest assured that it will be done. I will reach you to your destination safe and sound. And I shall drive like the devil himself to ensure that we speed past the amber lights without having to make any stops," the taxi driver replied.

Amar was afraid that he was being followed, and he feared that the taxi was being chased. And even though he wanted to ensure that he was not being pursued, he was, however, too frightened to look back, and he prayed that all was well. Fortunately for him; nobody was tailing him as no one appeared to be in hot pursuit of him, and he managed to reach home safely.

"Are you alright?" Jagdeep asked his grandson, when he stepped into the apartment. "You look very pale and frightened, and you look like you've just seen a ghost," he remarked upon noticing Amar's ashen appearance.

"I am fine, dadaji," Amar replied; and that, of course, was far from the truth.

Amar did not expect to be abducted by Gia, and he did not ever imagine that he would be held captive by her. And he never thought that he would live to see the day when he would be forced to marry her at gunpoint. Gia had stooped to an abysmal level and she had exceeded all boundaries. He never reckoned that his best friend would resort to terrorize him, and that she would succeed in scaring the living daylights out of him. And Amar was left traumatized by the terrifying experience that he had encountered. However, despite his trauma and terror, he endeavored to put up a brave front for fear of upsetting his grandfather.

"Are you certain that you are okay? You look like you've encountered an apparition. Even though you assure me that everything is alright, I can't help getting the impression that something is amiss. Are you sure you are not lying to me?" Jagdeep reiterated.

"Yes, dadaji, everything is fine with me," Amar declared.

Amar did not want Jagdeep to know that he was abducted and that he was held captive as the latter would be worried for him, and his grandfather would be concerned about his safety every time he left the apartment. Since Amar did not want Jagdeep to fret on his behalf, and have the latter's angst take a further toll on his fragile health; he thought it best to lie to his grandfather.

#

Gia was sent by her parents to live with a distant relative in Malerkotla, a remote town in Punjab, until the baby was born. They were told to provide her with a safe haven to deliver the child, and to accommodate her in their home until the arrival of her baby into the world. As they were a childless couple whose attempts to produce a progeny had proved futile and they had failed to have a child of their own, they would adopt Gia's baby once it was born. And they would be the parents to her child whom they would raise as their own.

"You are to tell everyone that Gia is your surrogate, and that she is carrying the child on your behalf. And no one should ever know the truth about the pregnancy." Jhanvi instructed the couple, and she swore them to absolute secrecy.

"Yes, of course. You can rest assured that no one will ever know that the child is not ours. And we give you our word that we will not sully your daughter's reputation."

Gia's benefactors assured Jhanvi that their lips were sealed and they promised her that they would not breathe a word about the circumstances of the child birth to anyone. And though they were curious to know about Gia's pregnancy, they, however, chose not to probe, and they refrained from posing any embarrassing queries. After having remained childless all these years, they were happy to be finally blessed with a child they could call their own. And they regarded the bizarre situation as a divine plan.

#

Gia gave birth to a beautiful baby girl one summer afternoon, and it was a natural birth. She delivered the child at home with a midwife in attendance to assist her with the birth. Her daughter was given to the adoptive parents shortly after she was born, and she would be raised by them as their own. And Gia would have no contact whatsoever with her daughter thereafter.

"This child is now yours, and you will be responsible for her upbringing," Gia stated, whilst handing over her daughter to the adoptive mother.

"You can rest assured that we will love her like our own, and she will never know that she has been adopted. She will receive the best care, and she will lack for nothing," the adoptive mother replied.

#

Gia returned to Mumbai after the birth of her daughter. And once she was back at home, she got in touch with Amar. "I know that I am probably the last person you want to hear from right now, but I'd like to see you. And it's important that we meet," she stated over the telephone.

"And you are absolutely right as I don't want to have anything to do with you ever again. You disgust me, and I can't believe that I ever considered you my friend," Amar replied.

"And I can well understand how you feel cause I know what I did was inexcusable. But can you at least give me a chance to offer you an explanation for my despicable conduct before you decide to sever all ties with me?"

Gia asked Amar.

"I'm making it clear that I am only agreeing to meet you at your insistence; and that too, very reluctantly. However, I can't promise that we can ever go back to being friends again," Amar reiterated.

"And that's a chance that I'm willing to take," Gia averred.

"You can come over to my place next Saturday when dadaji will be away. He is leaving for a pilgrimage to Badrinath early in the morning, and he will not be around. And as we have the house to ourselves, we'd be able to speak freely without the fear of being overheard," Amar said.

#

Gia arrived at Amar's apartment shortly after noon on the designated day.

"I am truly sorry for everything, and I regret what I did. Will you ever be able to forgive me?" She asked Amar.

"Well, that depends on what you have to say in your defense," Amar replied.

"What if I told you that I was issued a death threat? And that my life was at stake?" Gia stated.

"What do you mean by saying that your life was in jeopardy? And who would issue you a death threat, and threaten to have you eliminated?"

Amar asked Gia.

"Uncle Akash threatened to order a hit on me if I did not agree to marry you as he wanted me to have a husband before the baby arrived. And knowing that you would never be willing to wed me, I was compelled to have you abducted and get you to marry me at gunpoint. It was either our friendship or my life, and I chose to save my skin at the cost of our friendship," Gia said.

"And why didn't you think of going to your mother when you realized that your life was in danger?" Amar asked Gia. "I'm sure she would have come to your help."

"For starters; mamma was furious with me for dragging your name into the picture, and she wanted me to confess to having falsely implicated you. Had I gone to her with uncle Akash's ultimatum, she would probably have told me that I deserved to die. And I would not have gotten any sympathy from her," Gia answered.

"I can now see that you were in one hell of a situation. And I would probably have done the same had I been in your place," Amar said. He sympathized with Gia when he learned of her catch-22 situation. And though he did not quite justify the sequence of events that had followed thereafter, he, however, understood her conduct in the light of what he had been told. And he reckoned that she had no other choice.

"Are you still mad at me for having you abducted? And do you still hate me for holding you captive?"

Gia asked Amar.

"Well, I guess not as I can now see that you were helpless at the time," Amar replied. "And did you finally give birth to the child?" He asked.

"I gave birth to a daughter who was given up for adoption shortly after she was born," Gia replied.

"And I suppose you will be in touch with the adoptive parents to know the progress of your daughter. And I guess they will keep you informed of her welfare from time to time," Amar said.

"No, that's not likely to happen as I have given up all right to my child. And I will never see my daughter again," she said.

"And what about your parents, don't they want to keep in touch with their grandchild?" He asked.

"My parents never laid their eyes on the baby. And so far as they are concerned, I never had a child," Gia replied.

"Do you mean to say that your parents never saw their granddaughter?"

Amar asked Gia.

"Yes, I am afraid so," Gia averred.

"Does that mean you gave your daughter up for adoption without her grandparents laying their eyes on her?"

"Yes, absolutely, and that's exactly what it means," Gia reiterated.

"It's a pity really since the baby is innocent and she does not deserve to be punished. It's not her fault that she was born," he said.

"Well, what can I say as that's the way my parents feel. And they blame her for being born," she stated, shrugging her shoulders.

"Anyways, I'm sure you must be relieved to know that your daughter is in good hands, and that she is being well cared for," Amar stated.

"I don't think about her as I've shut the door on that chapter of my life, and I wish to move on," Gia declared. "The tragedy is that my mother ended up paying for my mistakes."

"And what do you mean by that?" Amar asked.

"You do know that mamma took a bullet when she tried to kill me?"

"Yes, I am aware of that. However, I didn't wait to see what happened next since I fled from the hall as fast as I could. All I could think about at the time was to flee from the place, and to get as far away as possible, before anyone realized that I was missing from the scene," Amar said.

This was the first time that Amar had spoken about the fateful day since escaping from his captors. And as he was still traumatized from that horrendous experience; he got the shivers when he recalled that dreadful day.

"Mamma took a shot at me twice, but fortunately for me; she missed on both occasions and I managed to stay alive. But unfortunately for mamma, the second bullet ricocheted off the wall before entering her spine. The injury left mamma paralyzed from the waist downwards, and she now moves about in a wheel chair. And she has been left an invalid post her shooting bid at me," Gia said.

"I am really sorry to hear that. And that must be pretty hard on your mother." Amar sympathized with Gia when he heard that her mother had become an invalid. And he felt sorry for Jhanvi for ending up a paraplegic for no fault of hers as she did not deserve to suffer for her daughter's folly.

CHAPTER 32

R ohit was dictating an important letter to his secretary, and he was trying to focus on the subject at hand when his train of thought was rudely disrupted by the incessant buzzing of the intercom. And he was compelled to stop midway, and pause through the dictation in order to attend to the incoming call.

"Rohit, good morning; this is Ravi here. I would like to see you rather urgently. Could you meet me at my office right away?" He asked.

"I am in the middle of an important letter which needs to be sent out immediately," Rohit replied.

"Well, in that case, you may proceed to my office once you're done."

"Yes, of course," Rohit affirmed.

Rohit had the letter typed and dispatched before he proceeded to Ravi's office. And once he had reached the CEO's Office, he was ushered into his room by his secretary, Dahlia.

"By the way Dahlia, could you please hold all visitors to my office? As this meeting is rather important, I do not wish to be disturbed. And since I don't want to be interrupted by the phone, could you please ask all the callers to ring back later."

Ravi instructed his secretary.

"Yes, of course," Dahlia affirmed, before leaving the room.

Once Dahlia had departed from Ravi's room, he took his private phone off the hook before turning to address Rohit.

"I hope I did not interrupt your busy morning by calling this meeting. I know that this is rather sudden and unscheduled. And I hope you are not inconvenienced by the impromptu decision to have this discussion," Ravi said.

"No, not at all," Rohit replied.

"Well, I have something rather important to tell you, and I want you to hear it from me first before the official word gets out. I called you here to let you know that I am quitting, and to tell you that I will be leaving the organization shortly," Ravi said.

"What? Are you serious?" Rohit asked Ravi. He was taken completely by surprise by Ravi's announcement as the CEO's decision to quit was very sudden, and it had come from right out of the blue. He had not anticipated the CEO's resignation since he did not expect Ravi to quit Stan Express Bank before his retirement. And Ravi Pandit was not due to retire anytime soon as he had many more years of service left before he quit working to lead a life of leisure.

"Yes, I am very serious indeed. And I'm resigning," Ravi reiterated.

"But why the sudden decision to resign since it seems to have come from right out of the blue?" Rohit queried.

"Well, to be very honest; my decision to resign is not all that sudden as I have given it very careful thought. And I've been considering quitting working for some time, but it's only now that I have finally made up my mind to leave the organization," Ravi answered.

"Are you quite certain that you don't want to reconsider your decision and perhaps even sleep over it before you put in your papers?" Rohit asked Ravi. "After all, you are giving up a plum post, and with the current employment scenario being what it is, you will probably find it difficult to get a similar position or you might even find yourself unemployed."

"No, I am not likely to go back on my decision as my mind is made up. And I know what I'm doing. I don't think I am making a mistake by resigning," Ravi declared.

"Well, you are the best judge. I assume you have got another assignment elsewhere, and that's the reason why you are quitting," Rohit remarked.

"I am not resigning on account of another job as I won't be working from now onwards. I've worked far too hard all my life and become a slave to my job. I'd like to bid goodbye to the work culture and finally do what I have always wanted to. And I would have taken this decision earlier had it not been for my children. Since I feared I'd be shirking my responsibility towards my children by quitting my job, I waited all this while before finally putting in my papers," Ravi averred.

"Does it mean that you're going to be unemployed from now onwards?"

Rohit asked Ravi.

"Yes, that's absolutely right," Ravi reiterated.

"And what do you propose to do after quitting your job?" Rohit queried. "And don't tell me that you wish to live on a farm and turn a farmer and grow exotic vegetables and fruits."

"Don't be ridiculous. And that's passé anyway. As a matter of fact, I propose to turn towards spirituality," Ravi stated, and he refrained from elaborating any further.

"I see," Rohit said. He was curious to know what Ravi meant by his statement but he, however, chose not to probe as he figured that the latter would have furnished the reason for his resignation had he wanted Rohit to know. Since the CEO declined to divulge the reason behind his resignation that meant he wished to keep it private. And Rohit was expected to respect Ravi's privacy.

"I presume Tanmay will be taking your place? And that he will be your successor to the post." Rohit stated. "Or, is the Board considering appointing an outsider?" He asked Ravi.

"Yes, you are absolutely right. Tanmay will be the next Chairman and Chief Executive Officer of Stan Express Bank. And, you will be taking over as the Managing Director from him," Ravi said.

"You mean to say that I am the next Managing Director of the organization. And has this been discussed with the Board? And have they given their approval?"

Rohit asked Ravi.

"Yes, of course, the matter has been discussed with the Board and they are in complete agreement with my recommendation. Incidentally, I have spoken to Tanmay about recommending you for the top job when the time eventually comes. You should find yourself as Chairman and CEO someday," Ravi said.

#

Nita was surprised to learn that Ravi Pandit had tendered in his resignation and that he would be quitting the organization shortly. And the news was sweet music to her ears. She was pleased to know that Rohit would not be reporting to Ravi from henceforth, and that the latter would no longer be her husband's boss. And that meant she would not be compelled to pleasure Ravi or be required to gratify him from now onwards, and that she would finally be rid of him.

"Have you any idea why Ravi is quitting the organization? And are you aware of the reason why he is leaving? I mean, did he mention anything at all to you when you were together last night?"

Rohit asked his wife.

"No. In fact, this is news to me since I had no idea that Ravi was leaving the organization. And besides, I thought that

Ravi would have told you the reason behind his resignation," Nita said.

"No, he did not tell me the reason for his resignation and that's why I couldn't help being curious," he reiterated.

"Well, I'm afraid I don't know either. And besides why would I know the reason behind Ravi's decision to quit?"

Nita asked her husband.

"Well, since the two of you spend considerable time together, I thought Ravi would have told you the reason behind his resignation," Rohit replied.

"I am sorry to have to disappoint you, but I'm not Ravi's confidante. And I am only his bedfellow who satiates his carnal needs," Nita retorted sardonically.

"Well, not any more. And you should be thankful that you will no longer be required to pleasure Ravi. Or for that matter; be his mate in bed," Rohit declared.

"And should I be grateful for small mercies?"

Nita asked her husband.

"I would be, if I were you," her husband retorted.

"You are even more despicable than I thought. And if that's even possible," Nita stated, giving Rohit a contemptuous look, but her withering glance was lost on her husband. As Rohit had grown immune to Nita's scorn, it failed to have any effect on him. And his wife's contempt was like water rolling off a duck's back. Nita did not know whether it was possible to hate her husband any more than she already did. Rohit was a vile person, and she was sorry that she had married him.

#

Ravi sold all his material possessions, and he donated the proceeds of the sales towards charity before moving out of Mumbai. And he relocated to Ladakh where he joined a Buddhist Monastery.

Pawang Monastery was a sanctuary comprising of 100 acres of land, with a serene lake and new woodland, and accommodation based around an old heritage manor. The Monastery was the residence of a small community of monks and novices practicing in the Theravada tradition. The monks lived as alms-mendicants, and they followed a discipline that was based on the guidelines established by The Buddha.

Ravi joined the Buddhist Monastery as a novice before taking the vows to become a monk. He would be celibate from now onwards, and he turned a total vegetarian. His thick mop of hair was shaven clean, and he now sported a bald, shining pate. Ravi gave up his Armanis and Guccis and other designer wear for a monk's robe, and he donned the simple garb of a holy man. And he begged for alms.

Ravi's day now began at 4.00 A.M. starting with prayer and meditation, and he renounced the material world in pursuit of spiritualism. And he devoted his time to God while seeking peace in his quest of The Almighty.

CHAPTER 33

Nita looked forward to her outing with Priya, and she had her afternoon well planned. They were to have lunch at The Taj President before proceeding to watch a movie at the Regal Cinema. The latest Shah Rukh Khan film had released in the cinema halls, and as they were both ardent fans of the Super Star, they tried not to miss any of his films. And since her husband was loath to accompany her to the movies and watch a hindi film which he termed as celluloid torture; Nita invariably watched the Bollywood blockbusters in the company of her friends.

As Nita had reached The President Hotel rather early, she waited at the lobby for Priya to turn up. And once Priya arrived, they would proceed to the Konark Restaurant where they had made reservations for lunch.

Priya showed up at the venue shortly after Nita had arrived. And she appeared to be rather flustered.

"Are you alright? You look pretty upset."

Nita remarked, noticing Priya's worried look.

"I'm afraid we have to call off today and cancel the day's program. I know how eagerly you had looked forward to the afternoon, but an emergency has just cropped up. And

I am sorry for this last minute cancellation, but it just couldn't be helped," Priya stated.

"That's a real shame as I had looked forward to our time together. Anyways what seems to be the matter as it's unlike you to cancel at the last minute? What is the reason for the sudden change in plans?"

Nita asked Priya.

"And believe me, had it not been an absolute emergency, I would never have let you down in this manner," Priya reiterated.

"Can you not postpone it until later?" Nita asked. "After all, it's only for a couple of hours."

"I'm afraid not. Mamma has been hospitalized, and I am required to be at the hospital. And that's the reason why I have to cancel today's plans," Priya replied.

"I am really sorry to hear about your mother. Is it very serious?"

Nita asked Priya.

"Mamma's appendicitis suddenly burst, and she is required to undergo an immediate surgery. And it is a medical emergency," Priya replied.

"That's a very serious situation indeed. And under the circumstances, you should have headed to the hospital directly instead of coming here," Nita said.

"Well, that's what I would've normally done," Priya replied.

"Why did you bother coming all the way here when you could have very well informed me about the change of plans over the phone?" Nita queried.

"That's because my phone died immediately after I had spoken to my sister. And as I'd almost reached the hotel when she called, I thought it would be easier to tell you in person about today being cancelled, rather than to stop to use a pay phone. Besides, I couldn't proceed to the hospital without informing you about the change of plans as I knew that you would be waiting, and it would be unfair to leave you in the lurch," Priya averred.

"Don't worry about me. You should be with your mother at this time." Nita asked Priya to leave immediately to the hospital without wasting any more time.

"I know the afternoon turned out to be a total disappointment, but I promise I will make it up to you some other time," Priya said.

"That's not important now. Convey my best wishes to your mother, and tell her that I wish her a speedy recovery."

"I'll tell mamma that you sent her your good wishes," Priya said, and she left immediately for the hospital.

#

Nita was upset with the change of plans, and though the situation could not be helped, and no one could be held responsible for the afternoon having gone awry, she was disappointed all the same. She had looked forward to having a good time in the company of her friend and she was crestfallen by the turn of events. And since she did not want to dine alone, she cancelled the luncheon reservation at the Konark Restaurant and settled for a sandwich from a street vendor before deciding to head back home.

Once she reached home, Nita let herself into the apartment as there was no one to answer the door. And after checking the messages on the answering machine, she proceeded to the bedroom.

Nita heard the sound of voices coming from the bedroom, and she found that rather strange considering that she was alone in the apartment, and that there was no one else apart from her at home. And she dismissed the voices as a figment of her fertile imagination, and she felt quite silly for allowing her imagination to run riot. However, when Nita entered the bedroom, she was bewildered by the sight that met her eyes, and she could not quite believe what she saw. And she wondered whether her eyes were playing strange tricks on her, and that she was seeing things. Shocked out of her wits by what she had just witnessed, Nita let out a blood-curdling scream which resonated deafeningly in the room.

Rohit was lying stark naked on their large four poster bed, and he had two nude women with him for company. The twins were butt naked with not a stitch of clothing on them, and they appeared to be pretty comfortable in their bare skin. The naked trio was engaged in a threesome, and they were going about their erotic performance with much enthusiasm. And as they were totally engrossed in their carnal antics, they did not see Nita or notice her presence in the room until they heard her agonized scream. Nita's ear piercing scream jolted them out of their carnal antics, and they became aware of her presence in their midst.

Rohit looked like he had seen an apparition, and the colour drained from his face upon finding his wife back home. Nita was not due to return to the apartment for at least another couple of hours, and she had arrived much earlier than was expected. This was not the first time that Rohit had indulged in a threesome at home, or brought women to their bed. In fact, he virtually had an orgy in their bedroom every time his wife was out of the apartment. He had, however, never had the misfortune of being caught before, and he had gotten away with his previous sexual escapades. And this was the first time that Nita had walked in on him, and she had caught him in the act.

Flummoxed at being caught red-handed by his wife, Rohit was tongue-tied and he was at a complete loss for words. And even as he struggled to regain his composure, he had no idea how he would manage to wriggle out of the situation he found himself embroiled in. He was well aware that no explanation would get him off the hook, and he realized that he would never be able to justify what his wife had just borne witness to. However, even before Rohit could summon the courage to come up with an excuse or attempt to offer an explanation to try and redeem himself; Nita turned around, and she left the room.

Rohit thanked his stars for not being confronted by his enraged wife but even before he could savor his good fortune, Nita returned to the room carrying a large carving knife in her hand. Rohit was quite certain that the knife was meant to scare the twins away as his wife was not courageous enough to use the weapon on him. Nita was too timid to resort to a murderous assault on her husband and take his life. And that is where Rohit misjudged his wife, and he made the grave mistake of reading Nita wrong.

Nita did not hesitate even for a split second and she did not think twice before plunging the knife right through Rohit's heart; and she was like a woman possessed. And she was in a state of frenzy as she stabbed her husband repeatedly. Nita did not pause or stop until Rohit lay motionless and still as his life ebbed out of him, before she finally resorted to pulling the blood soaked knife out of his lifeless body.

The twins called the police to report the stabbing before they disappeared from the apartment. And when the police arrived on the crime scene to investigate the murder, they were long gone as they had vanished from the place.

Nita was in a state of deep shock, and she was too traumatized by what had occurred to recall the exact sequence of events which had led to her arrest. She could only recall the memory of seeing her husband lying stark naked in their bed with two bare bodied women, and enraged by the sight that had met her eyes something in her snapped and she lost her mind. And Nita had no recollection whatsoever of what had transpired thereafter. The next thing that Nita knew was that the knife was thrust into Rohit's heart and he lay lifeless and still; and she was left holding the blood soaked knife in her hand. And that is how the police found her when they arrived at the apartment.

"You have the right to remain silent, and anything that you say can and will be used against you in a court of law."

The officer read out Nita's rights to her before she was handcuffed and arrested from the apartment.

CHAPTER 34

Nita was lodged at the women's prison in Byculla, and she now faced a lonely future. Her friends had deserted her when they learned of what she had done, and they had severed all ties with her. As they did not want to be associated with a murderer who had killed her husband nor wished to remain in touch with a woman who had snuffed out the life of her spouse; they had cut her out of their lives. And Nita became an untouchable and an outcast overnight. She found herself shunned by one and all who now treated her like a pariah.

#

Amar came to meet Nita in jail, and he showed up at the prison to see her.

"I'm surprised to see you here as I never expected you to turn up at this place," Nita stated, when she saw Amar.

"I could not stop myself from coming to see you," Amar replied.

"How did you even learn about my incarceration? And how did you know that I was lodged here?"

Nita asked Amar.

"Have you forgotten that I work with your husband? Or rather, I should correct myself by saying that I worked for your late husband," Amar stated.

It sounded strange to hear her husband being spoken of in the past and it was all so surreal since Nita could not quite believe that Rohit was dead. She was yet to come to terms with what she had done, and the truth was still to sink in. What had occurred was in a moment of frenzy, and Rohit's killing was an impulsive act. And as she was not in the right frame of mind at the time, she did not quite know what she was doing. Everything had transpired in such a split second that Nita did not have any time to ponder upon the act, or for that matter; to comprehend the consequences of her actions. And the murderous deed was a result of her fragile state at the time.

"Well, why are you here anyways?" Nita asked Amar. She strived to put up a brave front, and she tried not to let her fear show as she did not want Amar to know that she was terrified at the thought of doing time in prison. She feared that she might find herself incarcerated for life and leave the prison in a body bag, and that was a dreadful thought.

"I came to find out the truth for myself and to know what really happened. I know you are not a murderer and that there has to be a good reason for what you did," Amar said. "So, can you tell me why you resorted to killing your husband?"

"The truth is not relevant here since it does not change the situation. And I will be called a spouse killer anyways," Nita replied.

"Well, the truth matters to me. And I am not leaving from here until you tell me what drove you to kill your husband. The Nita I know is not homicidal and neither is she a murderer."

"For starters; my marriage turned out to be a complete disaster, and I made the biggest mistake of my life when I married Rohit," Nita said.

"How so, did your husband not love you? And were you trapped in a loveless marriage?"

Amar asked Nita.

"That was the least of my worries. My husband treated me like a commodity to be used in any manner that he saw fit. And Rohit used me to promote his career as I was required to gratify my husband's boss to ensure his professional success," Nita replied.

"And what do you mean?" Amar queried.

"Rohit forced me to bed his boss and to satiate his carnal needs, and I was required to be at his pleasure whenever the need arose. And I felt nothing short of a whore as I was forced to sell myself to Ravi at the behest of my husband," Nita elucidated, before proceeding to give Amar a detailed account of her carnal trysts with Ravi Pandit without sparing even the horrendous sadomasochistic encounters which she was loathed to recall. And as she recounted her tale of carnal horror, she was filled with shame.

Amar was close to tears at the end of Nita's narration, and he was saddened to learn of the ordeal that she had endured in her marriage. He realized that Nita had suffered tremendously on account of her husband, and he was filled with rage at the thought of Rao Bahadur ruining his daughter's life as it was he who was instrumental for Nita's miserable plight.

"I should not be saying this, but your father is wholly responsible for your miseries. And I hold him accountable for everything that you have undergone," Amar said. "Had it not been for your father, we would be together and none of this would have happened."

"Yes, and I could not agree with you more. And it's because of papa that I married Rohit, and it's on account of him that I was forced to endure my marriage."

"Why didn't you let your father know what was happening in your marriage?" Amar asked Nita. "I'm sure he would've done everything in his power to rescue you from your husband."

"Things were fine so long as papa was alive, and we were a happy couple. It was only after papa's passing that Rohit began to show his true colours, and I realized that he was a despicable human being with scant regard for another's feelings. Anyways, knowing papa, I am pretty certain that he would never have allowed me to leave my husband for fear of tarnishing his reputation," Nita replied."In fact, that was the condition upon which I was bequeathed papa's estate – the inheritance would be mine subject to my remaining married to Rohit and if I were to ever leave him, I would get nothing."

"Well, in that case, why didn't you ever tell me what was happening in your marriage? You knew that you could always count on me to get you out of your misery," Amar said.

"To tell you the truth; I was ashamed of myself and feared the consequences of you learning about my arrangement with Ravi. And Rohit held that to ransom when he found out about us to ensure that we could never be together. He threatened to reveal about my carnal relationship with Ravi, and he vowed to let you know that I was sleeping with the CEO to promote his career. You would probably have ended up hating me for selling myself to my husband's boss. And I couldn't bear that," Nita replied.

"And is that the reason why you didn't want to be with me?" Amar queried.

"Yes, that was the only reason why we could not be together because I never stopped loving you," Nita stated.

"If only you'd been honest with me, you would've been spared all this sorrow. And I would have believed you when you told me that it was your husband's fault you were satiating Ravi's carnal needs, since I know you well enough not to believe anything that Rohit tells me about you. You should have had more confidence in me."

"I never doubted you for a minute but Rohit somehow managed to convince me of otherwise, and that's what prevented me from coming to you. And I suppose I deserved what I got when I should have known better than to listen to my husband," Nita said.

"What happened to you was really terrible, and no one should have to go through what you did. However, it's all over now, and you should try to put the terrible past behind you and look forward to the future. Try to obliterate all the bitter memories, and stay positive."

"I wish I could erase all those memories but that's easier said than done as it's not that simple, and there's too much pain," Nita replied.

"I can understand how you feel and I know that it's difficult to forget the past, but you must make an earnest effort for your own sake. Anyways, I will be here for you from now onwards and you'll no longer be alone."

"It's comforting to know that I can rely upon you, but I honestly don't know if I can take up your offer," Nita said.

"I will help you get through this, and we can start a new life together once you are out from prison," Amar averred.

"There's nothing that I'd like better than to be with you but it's too late for that now as much water has flown under the bridge," she reiterated.

"What do you mean it's too late? It's never too late for anything in life," Amar declared.

"There's no hope of a better tomorrow for me, and I am probably doomed to spend the remainder of my life behind these prison walls," Nita said. She would have given anything to go back to the way they were before she married Rohit. However, that was wishful thinking and she could not run away from the truth. She was now a murder accused who was looking at a long prison term, and she was facing an uncertain future

"Nonsense, don't ever give up hope. And always remember that there is light after darkness." Amar endeavored to keep Nita's hopes high, and he tried to offer her some solace.

"No, there isn't any rosy future for me, as all I can see is darkness," Nita answered.

"No matter how hopeless and bleak the situation looks, it will eventually pass and you'll live to see better days. And I will be with you every step of the way from now on, and we'll fight it out together. I'll arrange for the best legal team to represent you, and they will pull out all stops to get you acquitted. It will be a long battle, but I'll stand by you throughout. And I'm sure everything will be well in the end," Amar stated.

"I don't want to get you involved in my mess as that wouldn't be fair to you. The legal battle is mine alone to fight."

"But then don't you see that I'm already involved," Amar averred.

"No, you're not because I'll not allow it. And I definitely will not drag you down with me," Nita reiterated.

"And what do you mean?"

Amar asked Nita.

"I know that you mean well, but I don't want you to try to help me in any way. And I'd like you to stay away from this place as well since I don't want you visiting me here ever again. I'm sorry if I come across as being rude and obnoxious, but I only have your best interest at heart here."

"I don't understand why you are trying to shut me out of your life."

"That's because I don't want you to tarnish your reputation by frequenting this place," Nita said.

"I don't care about my reputation as I'm only concerned about you," Amar replied.

"And I care too much about you to allow you to suffer disrepute on account of me. As you are the only visitor I expect to receive while I'm in prison, I'll refuse to meet you when you show up here next," Nita reiterated.

"Is that what you really want? Are you quite certain?"

Amar asked Nita.

"Yes, absolutely," Nita affirmed.

"Alright, I will respect your wishes, and I won't visit you or show up here again after today. However, remember that should you ever need me, I'm always here for you," Amar declared.

"Yes, and I'm well aware of that."

"Promise me that you will get in touch with me once you are free as I'll be waiting for you irrespective of how long it takes for you to get out of prison."

"I promise," Nita said.

EPILOGUE

The defense pleaded temporary insanity as the reason behind the brutal murder of Rohit, and he furnished the sordid details of Nita's marriage to illustrate her husband's infidelity as the final nail in the coffin that drove his wife over the edge. And he shed light on the circumstances which had led to Rohit's violent death. Nita's counsel succeeded in portraying his client as the aggrieved victim who deserved nothing short of the deepest sympathy.

The judge empathized with Nita when he learned about the circumstances which had driven her to kill her husband, and he opined that Rohit deserved to die. And he felt that Nita was right to punish her errant husband by resorting to execute him.

Nita was found guilty of the lesser crime of manslaughter, and Rohit's death was deemed as accidental. And the quantum of sentence was handed out to her accordingly.

Nita returned to the manor soon after her release from prison, and the years in jail had taken its toll on her. She was now frail and her health was failing fast as the prison term had cut short her life, and she would die much before her time. Nita wished to be buried next to her parents when the time eventually came.

Amar resigned from his post at the Stan Express Bank. His grandfather was long dead. Jagdeep had bequeathed his entire estate to his grandson, and Amar was now a wealthy man. He moved into the manor with Nita, and they would remain together until the end of their days.